About the Story:

"They had come so fast, the Lorsii, sweeping into the skies in their cloudy ships. Men had seen them coming and had reached out with electric voices to cry danger; they died with the cry still echoing on a million wires ....Died with fire in their lungs and disbelief in their eyes, as the stones of earth bubbled."

Jon Paterson had an inkling of their coming—but only in strange and confusing dreams. Josiah Crick recognized them as Evil incarnate. Ibrihim Zlotny, Servant of the Duality, Vicar of the Left Hand, Supreme Commander of the Army of the Final Testament, knew that with their help he soon would be undisputed ruler of the world. No one could stand against the power of the Lorsii, who exploded suns to watch the lovely colors and who wiped out whole races for their momentary amusement. No one except Josiah Crick—who knew that Evil could never finally triumph.

Crick's granddaughter, Rebecca, had a degree in mechanical engineering, and needed all her skills to keep their old freightliner (cargo 12,000 tons of protein from the Prudhoe whale ranches) moving at all. But even she balked at carrying that crazy man from the Alberta Experimental Station to the final confrontation that might—just possibly—save the world.

Apostle

Lovin's treatment of Zlotny and his army of dedicated devils is detailed and convincing; but his development of the nature and culture of the Lorsii is pure poetry. You can almost forgive them....Almost.

Apostle

by ROGER LOVIN

Edited and illustrated by Polly and Kelly Freas
Starblaze Editions • Donning • Norfolk • 1978

About the Cover:

The original painting, by Kelly Freas, is done in acrylics on illustration board, 20 x 26 inches. The left hand depicts a member of the Army of the Final Testament with a background suggesting his natural habitat. On the right is the lovely Lorsii maiden, Has-Ka-Vee, who has just discovered Earthlings, too, can make beautiful songs.

Large-size prints, without type, of this and many other science fiction subjects are available from the artist. For information write Frank Kelly Freas, 4216 Blackwater Road, Virginia Beach, Va. 23457.

First Printing

Copyright© 1978 by Roger Lovin
Incorporating a short story, "Apostle," Copyright © 1973 by Roger Lovin, substantially revised, which first appeared in the anthology *Flame Tree Planet*, Concordia Publishing House, April, 1973.

For information, write:
The Donning Company/Publishers, Inc.
5041 Admiral Wright Blvd.
Virginia Beach, Virginia 23462
Printed in the United States of America

Library of Congress Cataloging in Publication Data
Lovin, Roger.
        Apostle.
        (Starblaze editions; 06)
        I. Freas, Polly. II. Freas, Kelly. III. Title.
PZ4.L899144Ap [PS3562.0875] 813'.5'4 78-15252
ISBN 0-915442-61-2

Apostle

PROLOGUE

The old man runs doggedly across the ice. His shadow hops grotesquely before him, pushed by the bloody sun that squats on the horizon at his back. He is naked but for a bright rag tied about his waist, and sweat has frozen in his beard and the grey hair of his chest.

Spread in a fan behind come the gay boats on their spiderleg runners, pennants lively in the wind, sounds of music spreading into the bitter emptiness.

Every now and again one of the boatcrew will stand, furling its beautiful wings, and send an arrow to this side of the old man or that, turning him in his flight....

They had come so fast, the Lorsii, sweeping into the skies in their cloudy ships. Men had seen them come and had reached out with electric voices to cry danger; they died with the cry still echoing on a million wires. Died in ones and hundreds and thousands as the Lorsii sailed above. Died with fire in their lungs and disbelief in their eyes, as the stones of earth bubbled.

And the Lorsii had laughed their laughter like breaking glass, pointing with delicate fingers at each small agony below, as the flames of earth struck sparks in their jewelled eyes.

Here and there they plucked one from the inferno, wrapping him in cool forgetfulness and drawing him up through the burnt vapors to the great ships floating high.

And as they leapt through the endless night, they played their

1

complex games with the saved ones, so that when they came at last to the bleak giant that was their home, none remained alive save a single, worn, old man, the very last of the dreaming apes.

And they dressed him in gaudy rags and set him on the ice, coming after in their swanwinged boats to kill him. . . .

Now the old man slows. He turns to the shining boats and stands with his head down. He breathes raggedly; the wind snatches the white puffs and flies them away like lost memories. His feet are wet and red on the ice.

The lovely boats fold their sails and slide to a stop. They sit like patient insects in a crescent around the old man.

Three Lorsii come onto the ice and sail up to him on their bony skatefeet; their sailwings are like dark wine with the huge sun behind. They raise their curious bows, "Run, Man," one cries in his brittle voice. "Death is here."

The old man shakes his head. "No."

An arrow comes. The old man hears it pass his ear, singing his name in a secret voice. "Runnnnnn."

But he stands.

There is a movement on the boats. Comes a tall Lorsii, its wings set with rubies in patterns of power. It speaks with the three who came first, and they fold themselves into cones of translucent darkness on the ice, faceted eyes watching, watching.

The tall one speaks. "Why do you not run, Man?"

The old man stares at the ice. His hands hang limp at his sides. "Through runnin'."

"We end you if you not run, Man. Are you not afraid to end?"

The old man shivers. "Yeah. I'm afraid to die."

He raises his eyes, though perhaps he does not see. "You're going to kill me anyway."

More come sailing from the boats, tinkling curiously. They gather now like waves washed to shore against the old man's quiet.

The tall Lorsii: "It is bad to end. To end is not to sing, not to taste the wine."

"Sometimes it's worse to live."

There is a ripple among the Lorsii. Fluttering of thin fingers.

"How can this be, Man? All seek to live. Strong live, weak end. This is the game."

The old man laughs, his bony throat moving up and down, up and down. "You people murdered a whole planet for a game? Just for a game?"

"It is why to live, Man. Strong kill weak."

"But it's wrong!"

The Lorsii tilts its beautiful head. "What means this 'wrong'?"

For a time there is only the flapping of pennants in the hollow air and the reflection of the far, cold sun on polished, intricate things.

The old man rubs his sides. Heat is leaving him. " 'Wrong' means...means the reason you're doing something is not good."

The tall Lorsii makes a negative gesture. "Cannot be. We kill all. We live. This is good."

"You've murdered other planets?"

"Kill many. All we find. We are the Great People."

The old man tries to laugh again but only coughs. Pink foam flecks his lips. "Killed them all." He waves at the bleak plain. "And here you are! What are you going to do when you kill the last planet? You're going to be all alone. All alone. No reason left to live."

There is a rustling of wings among the Lorsii, pale light waving through thin membrane. Hostile eyes turn on the old man, perhaps unsure....

"Lorsii kill all. Kill you, Man!" The words kite away, paper-thin in the emptiness.

There are tears in the old man's eyes. "You can kill me, but you can't make me run. I'm stronger than you."

The tall Lorsii raises its bow and aims. The old man hunches his shoulders and shuts his eyes. But his feet do not move.

The bow is lowered. "You are strong, yes." The tall Lorsii turns to the decaying sun and wraps itself in its wings. "What makes this strong in you, Man? You were mighty warrior of your people?"

The old man shakes his head. The blood on his feet is freezing.

"Warrior? No. I was a—I was—something. Can't remember. I—" He raises his head. "My strength comes from God." His voice is resonant, and he seems, perhaps, surprised that these words have come from his mouth.

The tall Lorsii turns back and faces the old man. "This God is invisible master you make houses for, sing songs for? We burn many of these houses."

"He's more like a father," the old man says. "And a teacher. He gives us the knowledge of good and evil, gives us strength."

The Lorsii regards the old man a time, then comes onto the ice. "Tell us about this strong thing God, Man."

The old man's brow furrows. "Don't know if I can. Been years since I been in a church." Then he straightens, a kind of light in his eyes. "But I'll try. I'll try."

And he tells of the Creation. He tells of Eden and the tree of knowledge. He seems to grow as he follows the wild, bearded men of the Old Testament down the ages, walks with Moses out of Egypt, stands looking down on the land of milk and honey. There are gaps in the story: incidents lost, memories which refuse to come forth. But

3

the great story goes on. He tells them of the gentle carpenter of Nazareth, the man who owned nothing, gave everything, and was whipped and nailed to a wooden beam to die in agony.

Ice glitters in the old man's beard as he tells of the stone that rolled away, and of the Shepherd who walked again among His flock, dead yet alive! And of the eternal promise. Believe in the Lord thy God....

Now he stands, spent, facing the emptiness and the cold and the glowing eyes of the Lorsii. He draws a deep breath, almost a sob. "That's it. I'm ready now."

He lowers himself painfully to his knees and folds his hands. Tears freeze on his cheeks. But his voice is steady as he chants the old, old words. "Our Father, which art in heaven, hallowed by Thy name—"

When he is done, there is no motion for a time.

Then, abruptly, the tall Lorsii raises its bow and fires....

Later there will be whisperings in the language like crystal breaking and furtive meetings in the strange palaces. The story will pass in quiet ways and grow in the telling. In time will come the first of the symbols: a curious arrow pinning a cross. Later still, the graceful temples.

But now there is only the moan of the wind and the flap of boat pennants dying in the huge stillness.

The smaller moon has risen and eclipses a portion of the sun, making it look, perhaps, like an apple with a single bite taken....

The tall Lorsii folds its bow and makes a sharp gesture. "Back! The game is over!"

And they rise and spread their thin sails and go skittering across the ice like bony trees flapping in an October night.

CHAPTER ONE

Jon Paterson swam up out of darkness still frightened, still cold, still on an alien landscape. For a moment, the masked and goggled faces bending over him flickered in and out of reality; now the concerned visages of the doctors, now the glitter-eyed faces of...what was it?

"Doctor Paterson! Jon! Wake up."

Paterson focused, still shuddering. "Right," he said, trying to sound in control of himself. "Right." He sat up and promptly fell back again on the table. He groaned.

Two strong black hands lifted him to a sitting position and held him there. An ebony face came close to his. "How you feeling, Doctor Paterson? Can you remember anything?"

Paterson shook his head. "Something cold, Lee. Something—I think, I think something like praying mantises. Can I get up?"

More hands grasped him, lifting, guiding, and he was on his feet. He stood still while uniformed people removed the electrodes and taped wires connecting him to a bank of instruments. Someone put a paper cup of orange juice in his hand and made him drink it. It had the aftertaste of chemical stimulants.

The black man motioned him over to a control console where paper-strip printouts were chattering out of slots. "What do you make of this?"

Paterson took the offered graph, knowing that Doctor Hardin was helping him back to reality by asking his opinion, letting the familiarity of the routine pull him more firmly together. You're here, he was saying, you're a doctor of medicine just like I am. Read the EEG and give me your considered opinion.

But the EEG wasn't routine. Paterson studied it closely, almost hopefully. "I don't know, Lee. It looks the same as the last few. Peaks in the alpha seem a little higher."

Doctor Hardin pulled off his surgical cap and scratched vigorously at his greying hair. "I was afraid you'd say that, Jon. I can't find anything new, either. But look; we got new patterns on both the emotional and glandular secretion printouts. Why didn't we get a corresponding change on the EEG?"

Paterson made a vaguely helpless gesture and passed the printout back to Hardin. "What can I say?" He was a tall, powerfully built man who looked more like an athlete than a doctor, and his gesture gave him a faintly pathetic air. He knew this, and knew that Hardin and the others in the room were all watching him, weighing each move, each inflection of his voice, as if he were a three-dimensional version of the printouts still feeding into their baskets on the console. For a moment, he could almost see the huge, imaginary microscope hanging over his head and the label on his slide: Paterson, J. W., Specimen. He shook it off and straightened up. "Okay, let's put it in the computer."

Doctor Hardin flashed him a quick smile. "Right."

They moved down a long hallway: Hardin first, then a burly male aide, then Paterson, then another aide, and finally a straggle of technicians. It was all very casual, but the order did not change. Paterson stopped at a thermalglas window and looked through its iced-up panes at a thermometer mounted on the bricks outside. Everyone drifted casually to a stop with him, then moved off again as he did. "Cold out, this morning," Doctor Hardin commented. "We saw a bear a few hours ago, a small grizzly."

Paterson nodded to show that he was listening, knowing that Hardin's light conversation was deliberate. But his mind was already in the computer room.

The group entered the computer room, which looked like a small theater with a television screen as its focus, and spread itself through the seats, Paterson sitting front row center. Two technicians brought in the printouts and fed them into the plain grey box under the television. Two others went quietly to the front corners of the room and trained cameras and recorders on Paterson. Hardin sat beside him and signalled the room lights off. A small photographic pinlight illuminated Jon Paterson's face.

Hardin raised an eyebrow and grinned at Paterson. "You want to be Polanski this time or shall I?"

"Groucho Marx is more my style." He looked to the technicians and nodded once.

"Recording," one said matter-of-factly. "Standby for computer enhancement, sequence niner-oh-five."

The television screen phosphoresced. Scanlines flickered across its meter-square face. The grey box beneath began eating printout strips, growling quietly to itself. In the eerie semidarkness, hands carefully placed a set of electrodes on Paterson's temples.

Paterson eased forward in the seat, his hands gripping the arms. "Ah—" He watched the screen intently. "I think that stuff in the upper left quadrant is rounder, like a sphere. And it's closer to the flat part on the bottom. It's like a—a horizon or something."

Hardin's voice came out of the gloom. "Any idea about the blob on the right, the one that's moving?"

"N-no. Machine. Something mechanical? Something artificial."

"Emotional?"

"Yes. Fear, I think. It scares me. It's hostile. Or something about it is hostile."

"Something operating it, maybe?"

"Maybe."

The screen gave forth a repeating cycle of images, like a videotape loop. Grey on grey, blurred, as if seen through a snowstorm. The landscape of Jon Paterson's mind, translated into cathode tube emissions and enhanced by guesswork. And it was a distorted, nightmare view.

"Hold it!"

There was an almost instantaneous snap as a technician responded to Paterson's cry. The image on the screen froze.

"You see it, Lee? That thing in the corner that looks like part of the machine?"

"Mmmm, yeah, I think so."

"Can we bring that up some?"

The technician didn't wait for orders. The view shifted until a blur in the corner dominated the screen. "Best I can do, doctor."

Hardin was out of his chair, peering into the television set with his hands on his knees. The oyster-light of the screen on his ebony face gave him a sepulchral look. "What's Doctor Paterson's emotive balance right now?"

A woman monitoring Paterson's electrodes answered crisply. "Plus six negative, Doctor Hardin; overtones of fear and something I can't read."

"Jon?"

"I don't know. Recognition, perhaps."

"Feed that into the computer. Let's get a speculative

enhancement."

The assemblage sat quietly while the computer technician worked his board. An image came up on the screen, and everyone in the room recoiled almost by instinct.

"Good Christ," Hardin said softly.

On the screen was a face. A glittering-eyed, insectoid face, carnivorous in line and utterly devoid of emotion. A face which stared out at the small, dark room as if its owner were real, and aware of them.

There was a low moan. Jon Paterson had fainted. Hardin had the system shut down and the lights turned on. He brought Paterson around with smelling salts. "Okay, that's enough for now. Come on, Jon. I'll walk you to your quarters. We'll analyze this later." He put a hand on Paterson's elbow, but it was the two male aides who got him on his feet. They walked him down two hallways, while Hardin kept up a light, innocuous banter. Paterson had a feeling of *deja vu*, as though he, like the images on the computer screen, were living an endless tape-loop, but he knew that this was reality: the dizzy recovery walks were an all-too-regular part of his life.

They came to a plain office door, now standing open to reveal a pleasant suite of two rooms. In the first room were a desk and chair, filing cabinets, and a wooden plaque with the legend *Jon W. Paterson, M.D.* scribed on it in gold. The second room's doorway showed the corner of a neatly made bed and a dresser with toilet articles on it.

The party stopped at the door and exchanged small talk, and Paterson went inside, pulling the door closed himself. He tried not to hear the soft *thuk* of the lock being turned from outside as he stared through the bars on his window at the bleak Canadian tundra outside.

* * * *

The old man rocked back and forth, back and forth, humming contentedly. His bifocals rested on the end of his long nose, and he sighted through them, down the flow of his huge grey beard and across his rounded belly, as though they were gunsights. At the end of his arms, his stubby hands held a dog-eared, leatherbound book which leaked bookmarks like a sandwich shedding lettuce. A scruffy grey cat snored on his lap, its tongue protruding.

From somewhere aft came banging and thudding. An occasional *thump*, more solid than the rest, shook fine clouds of dust and ancient paint down off the bulkheads onto the old man's head and shoulders. He seemed oblivious of them, as to the series of *tap-*

tap-tap bangings which came through the bulkheads, repeated now with a definitely peremptory tone. He turned a page, nodding to himself as though in agreement with what he was reading.

The after-hatch flew open and struck the bulkhead violently. A grease-smeared woman in her early twenties came through the hatch, a wrench in her hand and exasperation on her face. "Elmer Josiah Crick!"

The old man started, almost dropping his book. The cat woke and went scuttling for the hatch. "What? Oh! Mmm, yes, Becky, child. I was supposed to be doing something, wasn't I?"

The girl threw her wrench to the deck and slumped into the copilot's chair. "*Grandpa*, you were supposed to try the engines when I signaled."

Crick nodded vigorously. "Right, quite right. I was just reading Carl Giers' treatise on Saul of Tarsus, y'know. Must've gotten a bit involved." He mumbled off into silence as he busied himself at the controls. The girl watched him with resigned affection. He threw switches and relays, then pressed the starter. Nothing happened, and he snorted. "Rebecca, fetch me my cane." The girl handed him a bent-handled walking stick. He reversed it and took careful aim. "Should be right about...there!" He whacked the instrument panel sharply just above the radar screen.

There was a flurry of sparks and a puff of acrid blue smoke. Deep beneath the deckplates, the big engines coughed and lumbered to growling life. "Praise the Lord," Crick shouted, smiling broadly at his granddaughter. "I believe you've done it again."

Rebecca rubbed her eyes tiredly, leaving dirty smudges on her cheekbones. "For the moment, Poppa-Bear, for the moment. We're running out of spit and bailing wire."

"Now, now," Crick chided, happily, busy at the controls. "Don't be discouraged, my dear. We've had our difficulties before. There's many a run left in the *Milk & Honey*."

"No, there isn't."

"Why, I was talking with Captain Van Tassel just last week—"

"That was last year."

"—and his ship's older than the Honeybucket by five years. He's—"

"It burned out last October, Grandpa, down in Brazil."

The old man went silent again, his hands resting on the steering wheel. Then he swung around to face the girl. "Yes, I know." His voice was sad, gentle.

Rebecca reached out and put her hand on her grandfather's arm. "It's over, Grandpa. This is the last run the Honeybucket's ever going to make—if we even make this one. We're still a long way from home, and half the systems on board are burned out. Even the reefer's shot! What are we going to do with twelve kilotons of meat when we get down into the temperate zone?" Her face softened at the look in Crick's eyes. "I'm sorry, Poppa-Bear. I just can't make her go anymore. She's tired and wants to lay down to rest."

Crick fumbled a blackened pipe out of his pocket and began stuffing it with loose tobacco from his jacket pocket. "Like her master, Becky girl. I've been sailing eighty years, now—"

"Sixty. You're only seventy-two."

"—since before your mother, God rest her soul, was born. Didn't give her much of a life, what with keeping her out here in the dark waters all the time." He sucked the pipe to life, shaking his head. "Not much of a life I've given you, either, you being practically born on a 'liner—"

"I was born in Tempe General Hospital, Grandpa."

"—and hardly ever seeing a proper school or church."

Rebecca laughed and leapt up to kiss the old man on his bald head. "Grandpa, I graduated in mechanical engineering while you were still first mate on the old *Gold Camp Runner*. I was seventeen before I ever got on a 'liner."

"Well," Crick said, as if not hearing her, "it's a hard life. It took my only child, and the best man who ever hauled freight."

"People get killed in any trade, Grandpa." She glanced around the cabin, frowning. "Did you hide the chessboard again?"

His eyebrows rose indignantly. "Me?"

"Yes, you. You always hide it after I beat you—which is all the time."

"That's not so! I beat you last Tuesday, right after prayers."

"That was last month, in Juneau." She spotted the board, carefully hidden under a stack of charts. "Come on, Grandpa, let's get the show on the road before we freeze to death."

"Right! Oh, yes, indeed," Crick agreed happily. He put the 'liner in gear as Rebecca flopped into the copilot's chair again and set up the magnetic board. "Queen's pawn two to queen's square four," he said.

Rebecca groaned. "Not that old chestnut again!"

"Chestnut! Just you wait. I've got a middle game worked out like you've never seen."

They argued and moved pieces in a kind of ritual bliss as the freightliner *Milk & Honey*, Captain Josiah Crick commanding, shook the ice off her forty modules and smashed south through the blizzard-swept tundra, her hundred and eighty three-meter-high tires sinking down to the permafrost as they rolled.

10

* * * *

The visitor approached at nearly four hundred kilometers per second, an insignificant speed when measured against the vastness of its environment. It appeared to simply hang there just beyond the orbit of Saturn and a few degrees above the planetary elliptic. In the scale of things, it was insignificant in mass, also. Perhaps fifty kilometers on its long axis, no more than thirty on the short, it massed less than a billion tons. It was sterile, as cold as the void it traversed. It radiated nothing.

But it reflected radiation. Its cratered surface bounced light from the sun, and some of that light reached Earth, where it aroused curiosity. Scientists sent probing fingers of radar, radio, television to explore it. And these, too, the visitor reflected back to earth....

"Woomera?"

"Tracking, Houston."

"Great Banks?"

"Tracking."

"Leningrad?"

"Tracking, NASA."

"Manitou?"

The radioman keyed his mike. "Tracking." The voice of the controller in Texas boomed through the control room, affirming the radioman's readiness, then added an "all stations on-line" and a warning that transmission would begin in thirty seconds.

In the back of the Manitou, Colorado, control room, a television newscaster spoke into a throat mike while his cameraman panned the room. "That was the confirmation from Houston, ladies and gentlemen. In thirty seconds, we will see the first live, color pictures from *SkyEye VI's* giant orbiting telescope, showing us the enormous meteoroid which is even now penetrating the outer fringes of the solar system. Scientists have dubbed the rock 'AV 346,' but laymen call it 'the visitor,' a name given it by its discoverer, the Russian astronomer Vladimir—"

There was a sudden commotion near the control room's main doors. A scuffle had broken out between the two military policemen standing watch there. As heads and cameras turned, one MP pulled his pistol and shoved the second out into the room. He leveled the weapon and swept the room with it. "Nobody move! The Army of the Final Testament is now in command."

Even as he spoke, the doors behind him burst open, and a swarm of hard-faced people in black and silver uniforms spilled into the room. They moved swiftly, with rehearsed coordination, and in less than six seconds had the room quartered under the muzzles of their weapons.

The newscaster's voice rose to near hysteria as he spoke rapidly into his microphone. "Ladies and gentlemen, it looks as if we've been invaded. Please believe me, this is not a drill or a stunt. I repeat—"

A girl of fifteen or sixteen, her blond hair pomaded into curving horns at the temples, strode up and snatched the microphone from the newscaster. "That's enough," she said. She signaled the TV cameraman. "Face me."

The man hastened to swing the camera.

The newscaster made a grab for the microphone. "Now, just a minute here!"

The girl sidestepped his lunge and stuck her pistol behind his ear. "Please do not make me kill you." She nodded in satisfaction as the newsman froze, half bent over.

She faced the television camera with calm arrogance and spoke in a high, ringing voice. "Greetings, sinners. The Army of the Final Testament is in command of this transmitting facility. Do not bother changing channels; we are everywhere." She looked toward the control room's double doors, where a measured tramping could be heard approaching, then swung back to face the camera. "Stand by for a revelation from the servant of the Duality, the Vicar of the Left Hand, Ibrihim Zlotny."

The doors swung wide and a squad of muscular young men marched in. In their midst walked a short, rotund man in a plain business jumper. He smiled benignly, as if enjoying a mild joke, his vaguely oriental face as bland and smooth as a baby's. He walked unhurriedly over to the newsdesk, nodding to the girl who had announced him, and took his place before the camera. His smile widened into positive merriment, wrinkling his forehead and causing his slightly slanted eyes to arch like chevrons.

"Hello, my friends," he said in a pleasant tenor voice. "I am Ibrihim Zlotny."

CHAPTER TWO

Lee Hardin sat crosslegged atop his desk, his eyes closed and his hands open, palms up, on his knees. The fierce winter sunlight beating through his window haloed the edges of his kinky hair, making him look more like a dark Buddha than a psychiatrist.

Jon Paterson stood in the doorway, unsure whether to break in on Hardin's meditation or just leave. Hardin settled the question by speaking.

"Come on in, Jon."

Paterson entered and propped himself against a file cabinet. "I thought you meditative types got insulated against outside influence when you communed with your navels."

Hardin stretched comfortably and yawned. "Swami Leroy knows all, sees all. I spotted you with my third eye." He swung his legs off the desk and dropped into his chair. "Actually, you clump a lot when you walk, thus disproving the old saw that big men are light on their feet."

"It's the intelligent conversation I get here. I am rendered spastic by the wonders of medicine."

"Ho, ho. Siddown, kiddo; I got some news for you." He shuffled papers as Paterson came forward and sat in the worn consultation chair. "Did Doctor Anderson show you the final computer enhancement on your boogiemen yet?"

"Yes, just before lunch."

"I'll bet that helped your appetite."

"Not much."

Hardin spread the papers as if fanning a poker hand. The top sheet showed a strange, winged creature, bipedal and upright, but possessed of four stick-figure arms. "Working off the assumption that the mental size scale is about the same as the visual one, we get a figure of two-point-oh-six meters height, and about thirty kilos weight, which makes your critters tall and skinny." He tilted his head at Paterson. "Who scares you that's tall and skinny?"

Paterson tapped the paper with a long finger. "Them, Lee." He locked gazes with the psychiatrist. "Look, I am a trained, intelligent man, with a sound background in psychology. I'm as qualified as you to assess the state of a mind, right?"

"Granted, with professional reservations."

"And I tell you, Lee, that these creatures are not mental displacements, nor hallucinations, nor even the products of a chemical or glandular imbalance—hell, I've seen my own charts!" He leaned over the desk, his face tight. "Dammit, Lee, they're—I don't know what."

Hardin leaned back in his chair, as if giving before Paterson's assault. He pushed his lower lip out and chewed it. "Jon, we've been through this."

"They're something else, Lee," Paterson repeated stubbornly. He sighed and relaxed. "Okay. Do you ever dream about food?"

"Frequently. I'm on a diet."

"And can you tell the difference between a food dream and the memory of a real meal you've eaten?"

Hardin thought about it. "Yes...."

Paterson smiled. "Right. And that's the way it is with these, these visions of mine. They're like memories of a movie I've seen, or a clairvoyant preview of something coming. They're—" he shrugged. "Whatever they are, they're not crawling out of some cellar in my mind."

Doctor Hardin pulled a pencil from his jumper pocket and began doodling on the papers spread across his desk. "Then how do you account for the fact that your visions—as you put it—affect you in the external world? I can't recall a single memory of mine which sends me into catatonia or epilepsis, nor even one that makes me go running through the halls of the University of Tennessee stark naked and literally foaming at the mouth." His words were hard-edged, but his tone was soft and friendly.

Paterson winced. "I don't know, Lee. If I did, I wouldn't be locked up in the rubber room of a loony-bin in the Canadian wilderness."

"Please. This is a research station, Doctor Paterson."

"This is the Alberta experimental facility for the criminally and incurably insane. I prefer my vulgarism to your euphemism."

Hardin laughed. "Touche." He pushed a paper across the desk. "What do you think?"

Paterson examined it. It was a rough but accurate caricature of himself on a pogo stick, desperately fleeing a roller-skated praying mantis. "I think you should stick to medicine. You've got a great future behind you in art." He skimmed the drawing back across the desk.

Hardin fielded it and held it up toward Paterson. "Look closely at these critters, Jon. What do you think I see in them?"

"An unresolved envy of Thomas Nast."

"Close! Close! I see an unresolved conflict in my dear friend and one-time colleague, Jon Paterson. I see a clear collection of phobic images—insects, glittering eyes, wings, bitter cold, towering adversaries."

"If you're going to tell me I have a secret urge to sleep with praying mantises, you're wrong."

"No, I'm not. I'm telling you that you've never made your peace with the old man on the cloud."

"Come again?"

"God. Jehovah. The Supreme Being."

Paterson leapt up, his face and neck reddening. "Baloney! I'm an atheist, a scientist!"

Hardin sat back, grinning hugely. "Pretty violent reaction for a scientist, Jon. And a pretty mild expletive for an atheist."

Paterson sat down again and fished a pack of cigarettes out of his jumper. His fingers shook slightly as he lit a filter-tip. His face was still red, and a vein pulsed rapidly in his forehead.

Hardin locked his hands behind his head. "Common enough, Jon. The first years belong to myth, no matter what intellectual atmosphere you're born into. Later, when you make the decision to run with science instead of magic, you're stuck with a load of guilt and fear for the rest of your life. Happens to most intelligent people, though usually not with such drastic results." Hardin was watching Paterson closely, his foot, under the desk, near the button which would summon the male aides.

Paterson lost his hunted look and relaxed visibly, feeling as though he were on an emotional roller coaster. "Lee, I know I'm not in good shape. I'm nervous and flaky and spooked by everything that moves. But I'm *not* crazy, and I'm not having religious nightmares."

Hardin eased his foot away from the button. He seemed to come to a decision. "Okay, old friend, I'll make you a deal."

Paterson nodded cautiously. "I'm listening."

"Instead of your hanging around all day playing guinea pig for us witch doctors, why don't you let me put something on that desk of yours besides girlie books?"

"You mean, go back to work?" He couldn't keep the hopeful relief out of his voice.

"That's what I mean. But there's a hidden duck in this deal."

"Which is?"

"He, he, hee," Hardin chuckled melodramatically, twirling an invisible moustache. He pulled a thick folder out of the desk drawer. "You been watching the news lately?"

"Patients aren't allowed. Too disturbing to their sense of reality."

"Only if they watch the politicians." He opened the folder and presented it to Paterson. "The chemically rendered and two-dimensional visage represented in that transparency there, Jon-my-boy, is of a gentleman named Ibrihim Zlotny."

"What kind of name is that?"

"A spurious one, as far as anybody can find out. Friend Zlotny appeared—probably from beneath a damp rock—a couple of months ago, bearing a message for earth's billions."

"Said message being?" Paterson studied the photograph.

"Said message being that lightning bolts from above had struck him and told him to go forth and save the world from righteousness."

Paterson reared back and glared at the psychiatrist. "Oh, no, you don't! You're going to try and psych me into getting involved with some religious fruitcake. That kind of therapy went out with the close-cover-before-striking schools of fine art. I'm not buying it, Lee."

Hardin ignored him. "Zlotny's touting what he calls the 'Duality,' appealing to the kids. One of his prime tenets is that the end justifies the means."

"I'm not listening," Paterson said, listening closely.

"WorldGov booted him up to us via the folder you're bending out of shape there. They want a very quick and very professional profile analysis on him, 'cause he's got them scared spitless."

"WorldGovernment? Scared of a religious nut? What's he got, anyway?" Paterson was trying hard to sound disinterested.

"For openers, a uniformed mob of neo-Nazis about two million strong—they call themselves the Army of the Final Testament. And for another, he's got NASA's Manitou, Colorado, broadcast and tracking station under martial law: lock, stock and personnel."

Paterson blinked. "What? You mean he actually seized it by force?"

"With laser pistols and stunstiks."

"Well, good Lord! Why doesn't the government just go in and blast him and his punks into greasy smears? Even if he's got the whole two million kids there, they can't beat the army!"

Hardin's smile held no humor. "Because before he took the place, Jon, his so-called army planted a couple of dozen pocket H-bombs in most of the world's major cities, each controlled by a fanatic with a deadman switch."

Paterson shook his head in disbelief. "I can't believe we've been sitting here for half an hour rattling about my problems instead of this thing. Why isn't the whole staff on this? Why hasn't something been done?"

"Zlotny just took the station twenty hours ago, Jon, and the whole staff *is* on it. Except you." He watched his friend expectantly.

Paterson jumped up. "Of course. I'll get to work." He was already out the door before Hardin could thank him.

* * * *

The *Milk & Honey* hiccoughed, wheezed, and expired. Her enormous engines strangled into silence. Puffs of filthy smoke blew out the sides of the engine covers and were sliced into grey ribbons by the hundred-kilo-per winds. Inboard, the alarm gong clanged once, then fell off the bulkhead. Every light on the dashboard went out save the emergency lantern just above the windshields. The temperature began to drop immediately.

Rebecca came swarming up out of the engine compartment through the deck hatch, a blast of freezing air and snowflakes accompanying her. "Damn and double damn!" she howled, half histerical. "That's done it."

"Don't swear, child," Captain Crick admonished. "Thou shalt not take the Lord thy God in vain."

"I wasn't," she said, almost in tears.

Crick peered through his gunsight glasses worriedly. "I wonder where Beelzebub is?"

"The mouse?" She looked incredulous. "Grandpa, we are a thousand kilometers from anywhere, our ship is defunct, we are about to freeze solid, and you're worried about a *mouse!*"

"Not a sparrow shall fall, Becky."

Rebecca stared hopelessly out the cabin's side porthole, which was already frosting over. "We're not sparrows, Poppa-Bear. They've got better sense. They're down in Florida right now."

Crick was busy at the control console, delicately testing circuits with his liver-spotted hands. "If the Lord can watch over sparrows," he said softly, "He will watch over us. 'Course, it don't hurt if we watch out for ourselves, too." He pulled a circuit board and probed among the IC chips behind it.

"There's no point working on the board, Grandpa."

Crick nodded, still probing. "Kahlil Gibran said, 'Work is love made visible.' I've loved the Honeybucket a long time, and I b'lieve she'll respond to that. Now, if you'll just hook this bypass circuit into the short-range and bleed the emergency cabin power, maybe we can hook the walkie-talkie batteries into it long enough to get a signal out before we burn off the tip of my cane—which I'm using as a sort of fuse." He looked at his granddaughter and smiled. "There's a hospital 'bout ninety klicks east of here, and we might can raise them on narrow-beam."

Rebecca frowned, then looked startled. "Why, you know, that might actually work. Poppa-Bear, you're fantastic." She grabbed a screwdriver and dove into the short-range transmitter.

"Used that trick once on the *E.R. Burroughs*, over in Siberia."

"That was Captain Carver, Grandpa."

"Oh. So it was. Maybe I used it on the *Asimov*."

"Hit the cabin power."

The emergency lamp went out, but the transmitter ready-light glowed feebly.

"Gramps, I think we got a signal. Get on the horn."

Crick took the microphone and harrumphed into it, straightening his shoulders. "This is Josiah Crick, Captain Commanding of the overland freightliner *Milk & Honey*, port of New York, registry number—"

Rebecca grabbed the microphone. "Mayday! Mayday! Anybody receiving please assist. We have lost power and are losing heat. Estimated survival time, two hours. Mayday!"

Crick rapped the transmitter with his cane. "I think that's it, Becky. The meters are at zero."

They sat in the twilight darkness as the temperature fell steadily, and waited.

And waited.

Rebecca looked out of her frost-rimmed parka hood. "Well, Grandpa—"

"We're not out of ammunition yet." He fumbled a well-worn Bible out of his wrappings. "There's a piece here just waiting for us to need it." He extended his hand and allowed his granddaughter to help him to his knees. She joined him on the icy deck, and they bent their heads over the Book. "The Lord is my shepherd, I shall not want—"

* * * *

The group was a blot of darker shadow in the alleyway, visible only through its slow, hesitant progress along the garbage-lined passage. Now and again, someone would stumble against a can, sending a clatter through the night, and the group would freeze. There were low mutterings and smothered, nervous laughs, but the laughter of strain, not of humor.

At the end of the alley, the group halted, faced with a bricked-up wall. A figure stepped away from the side of one of the buildings. "Follow me." The group went through a lightless door and down an equally lightless flight of rickety stairs to another door. This one opened to reveal a dim red light and a low passageway with pipes and valves along its ceiling. "Watch your head," said the figure who had led them down: a boy in the uniform and pomaded horns of the Army of the Final Testament. The group itself was composed of persons between twelve and twenty.

The passage went on a distance and ended against a solid, obviously new door. The young soldier knocked and was inspected through a peephole. The door swung open and admitted the group.

It was a large, cold room, at one time an underground parking lot for private vehicles, now filled with folding chairs, the majority of which were occupied. At the far end stood a small platform with a podium on it. Behind the podium hung a black banner. On the banner was a silver cross with curved, silver horns growing out of the juncture between the two arms of the cross. The curious symbol was slashed from left to right with a jagged, golden lightning bolt.

The new group took seats.

Presently, the soldier who had led the last group in mounted the platform. "Greetings, sinners," he began. "We of the Army appreciate your bravery in coming here tonight. It is unfortunate that blind and obstinate government has chosen to ignore and persecute the servant Zlotny, the Left Hand of the Duality. But it has precedents, for did not the government of Rome and Judea persecute the servant Jesus, the Right Hand of the Duality?" The boy looked over the audience, noting that there were many nods of agreement. He paused. "Your bravery will be rewarded, my friends. Your speaker tonight was to have been Major Hallaran, whose name you will remember from the Pretoria recruiting battles three weeks ago. But we are truly blessed this night, sinners, for the great servant himself is with us." The boy's joy was radiant, and he grinned at the murmur of incredulity and excitement which ran through the audience. "Sinners, I give you Ibrihim Zlotny."

Zlotny came padding down an aisle between the chairs, almost apologetically, as if he were late for something. Two or three people started to applaud but were silenced by stern looks from their companions.

Zlotny took the podium and commenced speaking immediately in his pleasant, matter-of-fact voice. "Good evening. Thank you all for coming. I can only be with you a little while, as the authorities are aware of my presence in the city and I must soon depart." He looked toward the boy who had introduced him. "Corporal, do I understand that these good friends are all novitiates?"

"My leader, this is the first time they have been in the presence of the truth."

Zlotny beamed and turned back to his audience. "Blessed are they who come in innocence to the thrones of the Duality."

There were a few "amens" and a few "nemas" from the crowd.

"It is written," Zlotny said, " 'Give of the knowledge of good and evil, that all shall know the freedoms thereof.' Ask, therefore, and I shall answer you." He smiled encouragingly and waited.

A girl in the middle rows raised a tentative hand. "Er, your worship, sir?"

"Ibrihim will do. Yes?"

"Er, I-Ibrihim, sir. You said on the TV that the world's gonna end. Is that true? I mean, like fire and destruction like in the Bible?"

"Indeed, it is, young friend. In fire and agony and destruction. The stones of earth will boil and turn to liquid. The houses of the mighty will fall. The unrepentant will burn and die, and burn forever after for their folly." He spoke as if delivering a humorous anecdote.

Another voice spoke from the crowd. "How's that going to work? Nukes or something?"

Zlotny chuckled. "Worse, sinner, much worse than that. The angels of the Lord and the demons of hell will walk among men. Their touch will crush, their breath will burn, their very look will make flesh peel off the bone."

A moan of horror swept the basement room.

A man in the back of the room stood. "Mister Zlotny, there have been doom prophets—false prophets, if you will—for thousands of years. How do we know you're not another?"

Zlotny beamed and silenced the angry buzz that rose from his audience. "A fair question, my friend, and one showing a skeptical mind. No firmer faith than that which has been tested; no firmer commitment than the converted skeptic."

"That doesn't answer my question."

Zlotny nodded vigorously. "Good! Good!" He searched the room and motioned a uniformed girl to the podium. She came, stepping with military precision, and stood beside him. "Captain, do you believe that I am the servant of the Left Hand?"

"Yes, I do."

"Why?"

"You smote my enemy."

"Would you explain that to our skeptical friend back there?"

She faced the audience. "A man beat me and shot me with a gun. The servant Zlotny lifted his hand to the man, and the man died."

A rustle of mingled fright and satisfaction went through the people in the basement.

The man in the back shook his head. "There could be a lot of explanations for that, Mister Zlotny. Sympathetic magic, drugs, hypnosis."

Zlotny turned to his soldier again, expectantly. She looked directly at the questioning man in the back of the room. "When I was shot, sinner, I was shot in the heart. I was dead. The servant Zlotny came upon me as I was being taken to the morgue. He laid his hand upon my breast and told me to rise. And I rose."

With a quick, simple motion, the girl unzipped her uniform blouse and spread it wide. A huge, puckered scar disfigured her left beast. She turned her back and dropped the blouse to show a matching scar just below her shoulder blade. There was stunned silence as she zipped herself back into the blouse and left the platform.

Zlotny raised a questioning eyebrow toward the skeptical man, and that man sat down. Zlotny raised a hand to the audience. "It is given to each initiate to know a miracle. As you join the Army of the Final Testament, you will experience the mystery and majesty for yourselves. That is the promise and the fulfillment of the Great Duality."

An older girl spoke up hesitantly. "I don't understand why you people have to go around shooting and killing everybody. I mean, what kind of thing is that? Killing is bad, isn't it?"

"Do you have children, young lady?"

"I'm only nineteen!"

Zlotny laughed along with the audience. "Well, have you a younger brother or sister?"

"One of each."

"What if you found them, one day, being threatened by a large man with an axe? And what if you knew that man was going to harm them? And what if you knew that the only way you could stop him was to kill him, and you had a gun?"

"I-I guess I'd kill him. But what has that got to do with your army?"

"It is written, dear friend, that all who are unrepentant on the final day shall burn forever. It is also written that a chosen person—a believer—can secure the soul of a sinner by bringing him or her the truth, by *whatever means necessary.*"

"Are you saying that if you shoot somebody, you're saving them? That doesn't make sense to me."

"It will. If the attempt of a believer to bring the truth to a sinner is honestly meant, that sinner is saved—not in this life, of course, but for eternity."

The girl subsided, still looking doubtful. Another boy arose. "I heard one of your guys say that you were going to give everybody on earth a sign, the day before the final judgment. You mean some kind of miracle like bringing that girl back to life?"

"A miracle, yes, but not like that one."

"Then what?"

"You must wait and see, young sinner. But I assure you it will be something which cannot be denied." He glanced at his wristwatch. "And now, I fear I must be going."

"Uh, Mister Zlotny. I have one more question, if you don't mind?" It was the skeptic again.

"Not at all."

"Well, you keep saying, 'It is written.' Written where? I'm pretty familiar with the Bible, and I've never heard any of these theories before."

"That is understandable. Have you ever read the book of Jasher? The book of Ibab?"

"No."

"Small wonder. They are Old Testament books, young sinner, edited out of the Bible in early Christian times because they did not preach the dogmas the churches of the day were trying to foster. In fact, they were early testimonies to the Left Hand, the first preachments of the Duality. Since then, others have been written, kept secret by faithful soldiers until these, the last days. They have been compiled into the Final Testament, and are available to all initiates."

The skeptic tilted his head to one side. "Just for us noninitiates, Mister Zlotny, would you define the 'Duality'?"

"Does that really need explaining, my friend? Can you not see that good and evil are simply opposite sides of the same thing? That one is pointless without the other, and that man, to be fulfilled, must experience both?"

"Then, you're saying that the universe is controlled by *two* supreme beings?"

"Equally."

And that the second, the 'left hand', is—?"

"Satan, of course."

CHAPTER THREE

Paterson jogged stolidly around the gymnasium, his pace less relaxed and rhythmic than it should be. Jogging was a physical mantra, nirvana through sweat and repetition; both a literal and figurative cleansing. But Paterson moved his big frame as though he were a soldier advancing on a stubborn enemy, and in a sense this was so. But his battlefield was a five-kilogram mass of neural synapses and his enemy was a traitor, a being of false information, half-glimpsed scenes, faulty maps, flawed campaigns. A traitor who never ceased whispering in a sly voice, Maybe they're right. Maybe you really are crazy. Electrons flowed, synapses opened and closed, and ideas were flung on the battlements of fear and uncertainty, all to die screaming and discredited as the perspiration spattered down Paterson's face, and the silent, interior war went loping around the room like a closed circuit tape-loop of futility.

Doctor Hardin stood on the deck above the gymnasium floor, mopping his own sweaty face and watching Paterson circling below. His partner, a squarely built woman, kneaded a handball and watched with him. "Do you think it's helped, putting him to work?"

Hardin nodded. "I believe so. He's been sleeping better since I got him onto the Zlotny thing, and he's not mentioned his nightmares."

"Yes, but look at him. He's not exercising, he's exorcising. He's still wrestling the demons."

"Yep. But I think it's the real demons this time, the ones out of his past." Hardin motioned her down the hall and into the locker room. "His father was very religious; one of those fundamentalists. He used to visit when Jon and I were undergraduates together. He never cared about Jon's grades, but he always wanted to know if we went to services."

The woman peeled out of her gym clothes and started the shower water running. "And did you?"

Hardin laughed, climbing out of his own clothes and joining her in the shower. "I did, mostly because I was on a congregational scholarship. But I think Jon was embarrassed at the idea, and I don't believe he ever went." He soaped the woman's back and turned to let her do his. "In fact, it was my remembering that which set me on the right track about his illness."

"It doesn't seem logical that his fear-figure is insectoid, though. I'd think he'd have more of a father figure."

"So would I. But Jon's an unusual man, and who knows what influences shaped him? He was already an introvert by the time he got to med school, and none of us ever really got to know him. I think I came closer than anyone else, but that still wasn't very close."

"Mmm," the woman said. She had rinsed and stepped out of the shower. She smiled mischievously and turned the hot water off, leaving Hardin in a sudden icy spray. He jumped out howling and chased her around the locker room, trying to swat her with a towel. She dove for the door and flung it open, then jumped back with a small shriek. "Oh, you startled me."

Paterson filled the doorway, his face a mask of deathlike concentration. Then he blinked and seemed to draw himself back from wherever he had been. His eyes took on intelligence and awareness. "Sorry. Hello, Lee, Doctor Marvis." He eased past them and began to undress.

Doctor Marvis exchanged a look and a nod with Hardin, gathered her clothes, and left, saying something about seeing them at dinner.

Hardin dressed slowly, watching Paterson shower out of the corner of his eye. "Making any progress, Jon?"

"On what?"

"Zlotny, what else?"

"Oh. No, not much. He seems to be one of those archetypical personalities who collects true believers. I can't see that he's any different than all the other Elmer Gantrys and Adolph Hitlers who've gone before him."

"Well, he's moved a lot faster than anybody before him—and more effectively." Hardin was not listening to Paterson's words but to his tone, trying to sound out the degree of interest in it. Was Paterson thinking or merely reciting? Hardin didn't hear enough interest to account for his friend's intensity. "What do you make of his religious schtick?"

"Zlotny's? What's new about peddling devil-worship? Or even a warped mixture of gods and devils? The Process mob was pushing that back in 1960. They put together a couple million kids."

"But their followers didn't become effective, disciplined soldiers overnight." Hardin tied his shoes and pulled one of his ever-present folders off the top of his locker. "Did you see the report we got from Madrid this morning?" When Paterson shook his head, Hardin extracted papers and read from them. "Says here that the zombies went through Spain in four days flat, recruiting a hundred thousand uniformed troops and God knows how many subversives. Says that they've got hundreds of documented cases where some teenager who previously couldn't zip his jumper without help became a drilled, military figure overnight." He snapped the folder shut. "Even the Turks can't make a kid into a soldier in less than two months, and they're the best unit in WorldGov. So how's Zlotny doing it?"

Paterson came out and toweled down. "I don't know. Mass hypnosis. Maybe brainwave feeders. Remember Scientology?"

"Uh huh."

"They turned out lock-step types in a couple of weeks on sheer ego-stroking, and all they used were tin cans and wire."

He climbed into his jumper, tugging against the dampness of his skin. "I don't think that's the question, Lee."

Hardin turned away to hide a small, relieved smile. Paterson *was* getting involved. "Then what is?" he asked.

"The question is not how he's doing it, but why. What's his motive? He's proven that he can field both an army and enough subversives to cripple formal government. And now he's got most of the cities under his thumb with his doomsday bombs."

"Harvard and Prague think he's planning on a worldwide political takeover."

"Won't wash. For all practical purposes, he's done that. He's got WorldGov by the short hairs, and all he'd have to do is say, 'Okay, now I'm emperor,' and he'd be emperor."

Hardin sat on a bench and dangled his hands between his knees. "That is the conclusion we've come to here. Most everybody, including WorldGov, agrees with us. Which leaves your question unanswered, as well as mine. Why is he doing it, and how?"

Paterson faced the black man, and the mask was back on his face. "Has anyone considered that he might be telling the truth?"

"How do you mean?"

"That maybe he really believes the stuff he preaches? That he believes Satan has a say in ruling the universe."

Hardin started to laugh, but stopped when he noticed Paterson's face. "Yes," he said carefully. "That's been considered. But not many people take that point of view seriously."

"Then maybe they'd better. Zlotny does."

* * * *

"Alberta experimental, this is land rescue unit *Moose*. Request permission to dock."

The switchboard operator scanned his clearance sheet. "Ah, Roger, *Moose*. This is a closed facility. What's your clearance?"

"Emergency four. We're bringing in the crew of a freightliner, the *Milk & Honey*."

"List your survivors, please."

"Crick, Josiah, Captain Commanding; Martin, Rebecca, first mate; Hezekiah, supernumerary; Beelzebub, supernumerary."

"Initials on the last two?"

"No initials, Alberta. One's a cat and the other's a mouse."

"Ah, he, hee, right, *Moose*. Bring 'em in through the south gate. Dock three, berth one."

The arctic rescue unit, a snow-covered steel tortoise, crawled through the electrified gates and docked. Station personnel ran out a weatherseal lock to the unit's hatch, and a team of doctors and nurses boarded. Crick and Rebecca proved mobile, if frostbitten, and entered the hospital under their own steam. They were met by Leroy Hardin.

"Well, Christmas has come early, I see," he said, offering his hand.

Crick took it and pumped it firmly. "They used to call me 'Bluebeard' 'fore I went white on the chin and bald on top. Thank you for taking us in." He introduced Rebecca. "My mate, Becky Martin."

"How do you do."

"Pleased, Doc. Nice shop you've got here."

Hardin smiled pleasurably. "We try. Where's the rest of your crew?"

Crick opened his parka to display Hezekiah curled like a belt around his waist, and Beelzebub peeking out of a pocket.

"No, I meant the other people."

"We're it," Rebecca said. "Have been for two years."

"Just the two of you, handling a freightliner?"

Crick shook his head and pointed toward the ceiling. "Three of us, doctor. The Lord's been with us."

"I see." Hardin gestured down the hallway. "Come, I'll show you where you'll be bunking. We're a little crowded right now, and very busy, so I'm afraid the quarters won't be all that much, and you'll have to fend for yourself."

"No problem," Crick said jovially. "We're used to a lot worse than this."

"Well," Hardin continued, "it's only for a week or so, until the blizzard lifts. Then we'll get a chopper up from Vancouver or Seattle to lift you home."

"Won't be necessary. We'll be getting back to the Honeybucket soon as the storm clears."

Hardin stopped, frowning. "As I understand it from the *Moose*, your ship's beyond salvage."

Rebecca saw her grandfather wince, and spoke. "No Crick's ever abandoned a cargo, Doctor. We've got half a billion dollars worth of protein aboard, from the Prudhoe whale ranches, and we'll stay with it until another tractor can come for salvage. Isn't that right, Grandpa?" There was authority in her voice.

Crick looked indignant, but subsided before her gaze. "Yes, my dear. That's right."

Hardin looked from one to the other, then indicated a nearby door. "Whatever happens, Captain, it's a week away. For now, you two—or four, I suppose—will have to share this set of rooms."

Rebecca looked inside, then shook her head. "Somebody's using these rooms. A Doctor Paterson, from the nameplate."

"Doctor Paterson is in another wing now, Ms. Martin. We're all working very hard on the Zlotny problem."

Crick looked puzzled. "Who?"

Hardin smiled, obviously impatient to get back to work. "It seems everyone up here is out of touch with the news. I'll send an aide around to fill you in and show you where to eat. Now, if you'll excuse me?" He was gone before either of them could reply.

Rebecca wandered through the front room and into the back one, examining the bunks and the toilet. "Grandpa," she called, "what kind of hospital is this? There are bars on the windows."

But Josiah Crick didn't answer. He was bent over Jon Paterson's desk, his knotty fingers spread-eagled on the edges of a computer-enhanced image. As he stared at the representation of the creature, the cold, alien eyes, the small hairs on the back of his neck rose. "Lord," he whispered, his voice shaking, "protect Thy lamb, for I am in the presence of evil."

* * * *

Ibrihim Zlotny sat in a bamboo chair, fanning himself with a palm frond. Behind him, the sun sparkled on the crystal waters of a shallow lagoon. There was a large, round table in front of him, with three chairs spaced around it. The chairs were occupied by two of Zlotny's soldiers and an elderly woman in very expensive clothes. This woman listened with the polite interest of the powerful as the younger of the two soldiers spoke earnestly. Without appearing to shift her attention, she gestured languidly and caused a dark man in livery to appear at her elbow with a frosted pitcher of martinis. With another gesture, she indicated Zlotny's glass.

The soldier finished speaking and the woman gave him a smile designed to make him feel as though he had accomplished something of great worth. Then she turned to Zlotny. "I must say you have a rather...charming theory, Mister Zlotny. I can see how it would appeal to the young. It *is* so much more fun to be sinful than sinless, don't you know."

Zlotny smiled in turn and sipped his drink. "Sin is a relative concept, Madam. There was a time when it was considered sinful in these lovely islands to withhold your physical attentions. Girls, in fact, were not allowed to marry until they had borne a child to prove they could."

"Quite so, quite so," the elegant woman agreed. "Of course, these were rather childlike folk in the days of which you speak, *n'est-ce pas?*"

"True. It took the French to enlighten them to prostitution and divorce, drugs and suicide."

"I believe suicide was introduced by the English."

"The point, Madam, is that it was an enlightenment, just as we are enlightening the world now. A step further toward unification with the Duality."

"I think you are playing with my poor grasp of the language, Mister Zlotny."

"Not at all. I am simply stating that the denotative and connotative values of the word 'sin' are subject to question."

The woman turned to the soldier who had spoken. "And you, *mon 'ti' vache?* Do you find what you are doing sinful?"

The boy shook his head. "No, *Maman.* Monsieur Zlotny has been chosen by the Left Hand to bring the truth to all of us in these final days. It is his work—and now mine—to save the souls of mankind before the storm of fire descends. What can be wrong in that?"

"It is truly a laudable quest, although I often wonder at the methods. I am reminded of an era in the Christian history; the Inquisition, I believe it was called."

The boy looked to Zlotny triumphantly, then back to the woman. "That was one of the prime manifestations of the Left Hand, *Maman*. There have been many in history. They have been sent to mankind to show us that even in the bosom of the Right Hand, the Left Hand has power and presence."

"How very interesting." The woman rose and took her drink to the balcony railing. She looked out over the sunlit lagoon and the red tile roofs of the village below. "I am curious, Mister Zlotny, about one thing."

"Yes?"

"Surely the work of saving all mankind can better be served from one of the more populous areas of Europe or America than from this poor little speck in the middle of the ocean."

Zlotny stood and came to the balcony railing beside her. "Who knows how mankind can best be served, Madam? I go where the Voice leads me."

"I see. Would that be the Voice of your Left Hand, or perhaps the voice of InterPol? I understand you are somewhat unpopular in many countries."

Zlotny's laugh was genuine. "I cannot deny that. I am proscribed, with all my followers, just about everywhere you can name."

"Then it is less the spiritual than the legal need which has made you prevail upon my son to offer you the use of my little domain?"

The young soldier popped out of his chair. "No!" The servant didn't mention it, *Maman*. It was the Voice which spoke to me, even as the Voice of the Right Hand spoke to His servants in time of need and made them give shelter to Jesus."

The woman's smile stayed, but it had hard edges. "Jean-Paul, I do not like the way you put yourself and your friend Mister Zlotny in that company. Remember that you are a Christian."

Zlotny moved between the boy and his mother. "Madam," he said quietly, "the boy now answers to a higher authority than you."

"To you, *Monsieur*?"

"To the Duality."

They stood, locked in will and gaze, and it was the woman who finally broke the contact. "Mister Zlotny, I do not think you will find this little island to your liking. Despite what my son has told you, I shall not offer you or your people the use of it. You will remove yourself immediately."

"No, Madam, we shall stay."

"Then I will have you arrested."

"By whom? Your village constable? Your household retainers?"

Something in his tone stopped her reply. Frowning, she peered over the balcony railing. In the village below, the streets were empty even of dogs. In the tiny harbor, the fishing fleet rocked at anchor; the nets hung limp along the booms of the boats. Even as she watched, a squad of soldiers of the Army of the Final Testament marched from behind a building and disappeared behind another. She turned on Zlotny. "So. It appears we are occupied."

"It appears, yes."

"And what do you really hope to accomplish by this?"

"The salvation of the world, Madam."

CHAPTER FOUR

Rebecca Martin came into the suite, her hands jammed in her jumper pocket and gloom on her face. "Of all the places to get stuck, we have to get stuck in a loony bin. I feel like a prisoner!" She went to the window and glowered at the bars outside. "Everywhere I go there's some two-meter-tall guy with biceps like a gorilla smilin' and tellin' me I can't go in here, I can't go out there, I can't use this section of corridor." She threw herself lengthwise on one of the bunks. "Did you know that the guy who had this cubicle before us is one of the flippos? They just let him out of his cage to work on—" She looked sharply at Captain Crick, who was sitting at Paterson's desk with his long beard brushing an open book. "Poppa-Bear, are you listening to me?"

Crick blinked and looked up. "Of course, child."

"Oh yeah? What was I saying?"

"Something about flipping pancakes. Are you hungry?"

Rebecca made an exasperated noise and bounced off the bunk. "Grandpa, we're *trapped* here! These guys don't even have a turbine shop."

"Ahh," Crick said knowingly. "Perhaps I can prevail on Doctor Hardin to let you have access to the station's repair facilities. I know it is hard on you, child, not having useful work to do. The monk Vistayama said, 'Without work, we are as—' "

"Grandpa, it's not that."

Crick closed his book and gave her his attention. "Then what is it?"

She looked embarrassed. "Poppa-Bear, there's no point in us going back out to the Honeybucket when the storm lifts. She's never going to roll again. You know it as well as I do."

He bowed his head slightly. "Yes, I suppose I do."

"So what now?"

"Well." He said it slowly. "We shall go home, most likely. You have a fine mind and quite a bit of talent, and you are an attractive young lady."

"Ha!" She pounced across the room and confronted him. "Just as I thought. You're planning on marrying me off, aren't you? You want me to quit monkey-wrenching and wear dresses and be some brainless little housewife."

He looked hurt. "Rebecca, that is an unkind thought."

"But true."

"Er, yes, I guess it is."

"Well, I won't have it, do you hear?" She stormed out of the suite. The real questions had remained unasked and unanswered, but they were at the forefront of Josiah Crick's mind. He was too old for another command, too poor to buy another tractor to replace the *Milk & Honey*, and too impractical about things like eating and keeping warm to live alone, as even he admitted. And there was Rebecca, whose degree in mechanical engineering meant nothing to her beside the reality of the big 'liners, who could not be happy except when she was confronting the fifty-thousand-horsepower turbines and rolling through the mountains and jungles of the world's ecopreserves, and who was too loyal and loving to ever leave him alone. He could not go, and she could not stay, and both faced the unhappiness of settled life with equal misery.

But these problems, serious as they were, occupied only the surface of Josiah Crick's mind. The Lord would take care of him and his strong-willed granddaughter as He saw fit. But was there time for that, now? Was there time for anything? Crick had spent his first day at the hospital station listening to the main topic of conversation among the worried staff: Ibrihim Zlotny. He had sought out the taped news broadcasts and watched them time and again. Then, in fearful excitement, he had gone to his scruffed and much-used Bible and studied it with a concentration he had never needed in all his long life of service to God. And he had come at last, in a kind of horrified ecstasy, to an unavoidable conclusion.

And so his mind, his heart, and his soul were now centered around the single question of how he, Josiah Crick, could be of use. What would the Lord have of him in these, the last days? For Crick saw in a multitude of signs, in everything from the expiration of the Honeybucket to the nightmare creatures of Jon Paterson's mind, and especially in the existence of Ibrihim Zlotny, the imminent coming of the last great battle for the souls of men. Through his mind's eye, Crick saw a flickering succession of his ancestors fading back through time. All had been sailors: of the seas, like Fear God Massey; of the void, like Phillip Crick of the Jupiter expeditions; of the wilderness, like his father and grandfather before him. And all had been men of God. Some in quiet, personal faith, and some, like Crick himself, as bearers of the Word, lay or ordained messengers of the Good News who took the Word with them in their ships and gave it to the people in the far ports of call, the way stations, the nooks and crannies of the earth and the sky. In his memory's eye, Crick saw all these men who had gone before him waiting in complete belief for the battle, each armed in the Lord and prepared for use. And he was for a moment overwhelmed that it was he who would be the last of the line, the culmination of all those centuries of prayer and preparedness. That he, old and used up and perhaps a little senile, should be the one to stand for all those men at Armageddon.

* * * *

"This?"

"Butterflies."

"And this?"

"A factory."

"How about this one?"

Paterson grunted and stood up. "I'm sorry, son. I've given too many Rorschachs myself. I can't be dispassionate enough to keep from loading my answers."

The pimply faced intern twitched nervously. "I thought so. You're too normal in your responses." He reddened. "I'm sorry, Doctor. I didn't mean to imply that you weren't normal."

"Relax. If I were, I'd be sitting in your chair."

The boy displayed his gratitude. "It's not easy, working on—with—someone who knows how the tests work."

"And who shall guard the guardians."

"Yes, something like that. Maybe we need some research on how to test the guys who write the tests?" He bundled the inkblots into an untidy heap and clutched them to his bosom. "Well, now," he said briskly, edging toward the door. "I think we've—"

"Made some progress," Paterson finished. "Don't worry about a thing. Take two aspirin and call me in the morning."

The intern flushed again and looked resentful. "I'm just doing my job, Doctor." He left in a huff.

Paterson watched his retreating back, wondering in passing about the decline and fall of medicine. He patted his jumper for a cigarette, feeling suddenly depressed, and found he was out. Could he get into the commissary on bluff, hoping his temporary staff status would override his permanent position of resident lunatic? He set off for the staff lounge, knowing he could get cigarettes by pretty-pleasing the ward aide, but resenting the implications of doing so. Loony or not, he was a grown man and capable of poisoning his own lungs without asking permission.

He passed a bulletin board, registering it peripherally. The usual daynotes had been replaced now by incoming data on the Zlotny crises. A wag had pinned a banner across the top of the board, reading, "Zombies 10, WorldGov 0."

Zlotny. The name kept clanging through his head as though in cacophonous counterpoint to the steady, crushing rhythm of his own inner terrors. He began to bounce it in his head in time to his footsteps, knowing it was mental chewing gum designed to keep him from confronting the Lorsii.

He stopped dead in his tracks, a chill running through him. Lorsii? Lorsii? Where had that name come from? But he knew without really knowing how. It was the name of the creatures in his dream; the generic name. And the blurred, foggy images in his mind took on a slightly sharper focus. A fact here, an understanding there. The bright spots in the wings were jewels. Surgically implanted emblems of position and status. The flatness underfoot was ice, a vast windswept plain of ice. The vehicles were... were.... He lost it. Boats? Iceboats? What?

All the while, the beat coursed through his skull. Zlotny/ Lorsii, Zlotny/Lorsii.

"Can I help you, sir?"

He had been walking, unaware, and was at the door to the lounge. A short, muscular aide blocked the entrance deferentially but firmly. Paterson cleared his throat. "No, thank you. I'm just having coffee and getting some smokes." He tried for his quietly authoritative tone.

"I believe you are a patient, aren't you, sir? Patients are not permitted in the staff commissary."

Paterson put on an indulgent face. "I've been transferred to staff. Check with Doctor Hardin if you wish." The aide still looked dubious, and Paterson gave what he hoped was a sincere grin. "Don't worry. If I start climbing the walls you can come for me with the net."

The aide weighed him a moment, then stepped aside. "Don't

worry, Doctor; I will." His own smile was about as sincere as Paterson's, and it was clear that he would do just that if it proved necessary.

Paterson went in and bought coffee and smokes, asking that it be charged to Hardin rather than having to present his patient's chit. He held the steaming plastic cup gingerly by a thumb and finger and made his way to a table by a window, wondering if he'd chosen that spot because the windows here didn't have bars on them. Zlotny/Lorsii, Zlotny/Lorsii. Was there a connection he was missing, or was he spinning his wheels? Why had the name popped up? What had he done or thought or felt that pulled that data-bit out of his subconscious? Could he do it again?

"Hello, mind if I join you?"

Paterson looked up to see a tall, windburned girl smiling hesitantly down at him. He straightened in his chair and returned the smile. "By all means."

Rebecca sat and extended her hand. "Rebecca Martin."

"Jon Paterson," he said, returning her handshake. Her grip was pleasantly firm, and he could feel calluses on her palms.

"Paterson? I've heard that somewhere. Are you on the staff?"

"Off and on. You're new here?"

"Yes. I mean, no. I mean I don't work here."

"Surely you're not sightseeing all the way out here in the tundra?"

"Not hardly. I'm first mate on my grandfather's freightliner, the *Milk & Honey*. We blew both engines a hundred klicks west of here and had to be rescued by a crawler."

"Tough luck," Paterson said sympathetically, sipping his coffee. "I guess that does in your profit for this run."

"This run was supposed to pay for the *last* run's repairs. And this time the Honeybucket's beyond repair." She shook her head. "This time, she's doornail dead."

Paterson saw the hurt and frustration in her face and saw that it went deeper than the problem of a broken machine. He looked at her more closely, noticing the cracked knuckles and dirt-caked fingernails of her slim hands and the premature lines that constant worry was beginning to put in her forehead. She looked, he thought, exactly like the girls of his own childhood, wearing themselves old on the hardscrabble dirt farms of the Tennessee mountains, always one step behind enough to eat and one step ahead of bankruptcy. Until the day came when they stumbled, and the family drifted off in a rattletrap old steamer with blackened pots and sagging mattresses strapped on it, to seek employment in the mills of Knoxville or the fields of the Georgia AgriPlex. Sunset came at noon in their lives.

Paterson offered her a cigarette. "The 'liner was all you and your grandfather had, wasn't it?"

She smiled ruefully. "For all practical purposes. Poppa-Bear's got faith, and I've got a degree in mechanical engineering, but the 'liners are all we've ever known. Now he's too old to get hired and too broke to buy another rig."

"And you're too fond of him to leave."

She made a helpless gesture. "He's got nobody else and neither have I."

They sat silent for a minute or so, just looking at each other. Paterson saw that beneath the fatigue and worry she was an attractive young woman. Not pretty, but the kind of woman who would age well and come to be considered handsome. Her square jaw and steady grey eyes indicated an underlying strength of character, or possibly stubbornness, which he found appealing. If her chestnut hair were cleaner and combed, he thought, it would be beautiful. Abruptly, he wondered what sort of children she would produce.

Rebecca's inspection of Paterson was more intuitive than analytic. She noted the surface details—dark, brooding eyes; thick blond hair going grey at the sides; blunt nose over a mouth a little too wide for the face—but drew her conclusions from more subtle things like the set of his powerful shoulders and the way his long-fingered hands toyed with his cigarette and coffee cup. She felt him radiate a kind of heat made up of conflicts and passions, and decided that he was like a large, strong animal of uncertain intentions; attractive but potentially destructive. Abruptly, she wondered what kind of children he would produce.

They both blushed simultaneously, each conscious of the other's physical presence. Paterson hid behind his coffee, and Rebecca brushed invisible lint from her jumper. The motion drew both their attentions to her small, high breasts, the nipples of which promptly stiffened to show through the thin fabric, and each blushed again.

Paterson cleared his throat and spoke, his voice coming out as a high squeak. "What are—mmmph." He got his vocal cords under control. "What are you and your grandfather going to do now, Miss Martin?"

"I don't really know. We'll be here two more days, I figure—till the blizzard lets up. Then I've got to distract him."

"From what?"

"Poppa-Bear's quite religious, and he's got it into his head that he's meant to singlehandedly trounce this Zlotny guy. If I don't find some other direction for him, he'll try it."

"Maybe he'd succeed. Somebody's got to stop him and none of the rest of us are doing much good."

"The captain's seventy-two years old and forgets to put his socks on half the time."

"Never understimate the power of faith, Miss Martin."

She made a scolding sound. "You sound just like him! He's forever quoting scripture or philosophic homilies at me. He's got a parable for everything."

"Perhaps he has one for Zlotny."

"A curse would be more appropriate."

The physical tension was still between them, and Rebecca's mention of Zlotny had brought back Paterson's tape-loop: Zlotny/Lorsii, Zlotny/Lorsii. Now it had a disturbing new element. Zlotny/Lorsii/The Captain. He felt the room pressing in on him and strove to change the subject. "What are you doing to distract your grandfather?"

Unaware of her companion's inner struggle, she replied moodily. "I'm trying to do an about-face and convince him that we can get the Honeybucket home again somehow. I'm hoping that will keep him occupied; he's amazingly good at thinking up solutions to impossible problems. He's been sailing since the days when it was trucks instead of 'liners and invented half the tricks the old hands know."

Paterson was trying hard to maintain a conversational face, but losing ground. There was a constant pounding in his head, a brazen gonging of something clamoring to get free. He had a seasick feeling and knew with awful certainty that he was minutes away from an epileptic seizure. He stood up awkwardly.

"Well, Miss Martin," he said, not completely able to keep the strain out of his voice. "It's been pleasant, but I have to get back to w-work. I'll see you around the station, okay?"

She stood with him. "Sure. Say, are you all right? You look like you're going to faint."

"Touch of flu. Still getting over it." Over it/over it/over it. He was hollow inside, echoing and floating away. The girl receded and rushed at him alternately.

"If you get a chance, stop by and meet Grandpa. We're bunking in the patient's wing, in some fruitcake doctor's quart—oh." She remembered where she'd seen his name. "I'm sorry."

But Paterson wasn't there to accept the apology. His body was staggering down the hall outside the commissary, and his mind was on a bitter-cold plain, watching a line of graceful, deadly boats sailing down on him, their pennants snapping like whipcracks in the endless air.

CHAPTER FIVE

Hardin was running data through the analyzer when the nurse burst in. Knowing her for a non-precipitous sort, he was already flipping switches to "off" before she spoke. "Yes?"

"It's Doctor Paterson, sir. I think you'd better come."

Hardin's pace was just short of a jog as he sliced across the hospital to the emergency unit. He scattered orders and technicians in all directions. "Where did they find him?"

"In a cleaning station."

"Catatonic?"

"Epileptic."

"Did anyone think to record?"

"Uh, no, sir, not that I know of."

"Then get the person who found him on tape. I want to know what he said, his position, his metabolic rate if anyone thought to take it—everything. I want to know what set it off this time."

"He was apparently in the doctor's lounge, sir."

"With whom?"

"That civilian girl the rescue unit brought in."

"Tape her. I'll want to interview her after I see Jon."

They had arrived at the emergency room, and Hardin, familiar as he was with the scene, felt as though he had stepped into a page from the *Purgatorio*. Paterson was on an operating table, covered with blood and vomit. Five or six technicians were trying to hold him down as he shook and screamed. One of the big male nurses was bleeding at the nose. They had managed to get several electrodes taped to Paterson's head and body, and one of the four restraining straps was more or less in place. But it was still a toss-up as to whether they would get the rest of them on before he burst free and wrought havoc.

Doctor Hardin went to Paterson's side and calmly took his pulse. "You've not given him anything, have you? No sedatives?"

"No, sir."

"Good. Let's get the computers hooked in. His pulse is holding steady, and I don't think he's in trouble. Phil?"

"Sir?"

"Get an audio going and let's see if he can hear what he said the last time."

"Right."

"Drucker, aren't you the nurse who knows acupressure?"

"Yes, Doctor, I am."

"See if you can calm him a little. You might try the left medial nerve, right about there."

"Audio's on-line, Doctor."

"Okay, give nurse Drucker a moment, then cut it in."

The nurse, a petite woman with protuberant ears, applied pressure to Paterson's medial nerve in short, sharp jabs of her knuckle followed by a stroking motion. After a few seconds, Paterson's struggles grew weaker and he relaxed visibly, though still twitching. His cries of terror became moans, and his eyes, while still not seeing the emergency room, lost the blindness that had been on them.

"Now," Hardin said.

A small speaker crackled. A voice came out, distorted but recognizable as Paterson's. "Dark," it said, flat and monotonous. "Dark. Cold. Something—moving. Toward me, coming at me, coming to get me. Coming for all of us but I'm the last there's no one left oh God oh God don't let them get me please please pleeease!" The voice rose to a high-pitched screech, piteous and terrified, and deteriorated into babble.

Hardin watched Paterson closely, recording in his trained mind the minutest flickers of his eyelids, the tiniest twitches of his cheeks.

Suddenly, Paterson opened his eyes and sat up as far as the restraining strap would let him. He looked at Hardin with every appearance of rationality and shook his head. "That's not it, Lee. That's not the way it is, there."

Hardin exchanged glances with the rest of the people in the room, then faced Paterson. "Are you awake, Jon?"

Paterson untied the restraining strap and got off the table. "Yes, though I'm not sure I want to be. Let's go to your office." He walked out of the room without looking back, leaving the roomful of medical people nonplussed. Hardin looked around. "Well, what do you think? Is he really awake or is this a new manifestation of his subconscious?"

There was a murmur of uncertainty. Hardin did not appear to really be listening for answers. "Get the tape of this last few minutes into analysis and ready for me. I'll go to Jon."

The nurse with the bloody nose stepped up. "Shall I come with you?"

"No, I think not. I'll hit the panic button if it proves necessary." Slowly, as if walking a minefield, the doctor followed his possibly rational, possibly dangerous patient to his office.

* * * *

Josiah Crick was bent over his desk, elbow deep in scribbled paper and schematics and with a pencil sticking out of his flowing beard, when Rebecca came in. He beamed at her. "Ah, there you are, child! Where've you been?"

"Sticking my foot in my mouth," she replied sourly. "Is there any cocoa left?"

"On the sink. Listen, Becky—"

"You know that guy whose quarters we're in, that Doctor Paterson?"

Crick sat back, becoming aware of her mood. "What about him?"

"I had coffee with him in the station gedunk. Everything was fine till I said or did something wrong; then he turned white and got up and ran. He had some kind of fit, and they had to come and take him away." There was hurt and fear in her face. "He was so, so normal, Poppa-Bear, right up until the last."

Crick saw his granddaughter stripped of her years of training and living in the artificial, masculine world of the 'liners; saw her once again as a very young person confronting a new and frightening thing. He knew she could handle the roughest of rough men, giving as good as she got, and that nothing in God's natural world could shake her. But she had looked on one of Satan's faces this day, had seen the Holiness of God's finest creation, the human brain, befouled by disease. "In all cultures and all ages, Becky, the insane have been regarded as holy. Have you ever stopped to think why?"

"No."

"Because they are of us but not like us, and because they remind us of the terrible mystery of God. We look upon suffering and wonder why God lets it happen, but we learn that suffering has its values and is often the tool God uses to cleanse our souls." He swept the room in an inclusive gesture. "A place like this, child; it is a testing ground for the best that is in us, for it is the collecting place of God's ultimate sufferers. Without the mind, what are we?"

She shuddered but did not answer.

"But God is just, Becky, and His hand touches the afflicted. He reminds us that we are kin to them, and that they are His children even as we are, by speaking through them. It is many times the insane who see most clearly, and in their innocence become the mouths of the Almighty."

Rebecca got up and made herself a cup of cocoa, still brooding. "I don't understand what you're saying, Grandpa."

"I am saying, do not fear Doctor Paterson's difference, but cherish it. It is easy to love the bright and beautiful, but more worthwhile to love the unlovely or the—ill." He studied her face to see if he had succeeded in shifting her fear toward the more easily handled question of morality. And it appeared that he had. He beamed at her again. "Now, come look what I've figured out!" He removed Hezekiah from the litter of papers and pulled the pencil out of his beard. "What's the ground clearance under the tractor?"

"Two meters," she said, knowing that he knew the figure himself but allowing herself to be pulled into his conversation anyway.

"Right. Now, suppose we torched the mounts and dropped the turbines *plop*, right out in the snow? That'd gain us a weight reduction of eleven tons. Then, we pull the steering servos off the two rear freight modules and mount them on the tractor. That gives us—"

"Grandpa, what are you talking about?"

"—power on both the drive axles. If you can convert the reefer generator to direct current, we could power the tractor and pull one of the fuel modules. We'd only make about a kilo and a half per hour, but—"

"Poppa-Bear! You're not seriously thinking about trying to run the Honeybucket out under her own steam?"

"Yep. The company'll send another tractor up for the freight."

She shook her head violently. "Uh-*uh*. There's no point in it. Even if we could get her moving again, which I seriously doubt, what would we accomplish? We'd be back home with just what we've got here—a dead tractor. And if she gave out somewhere along the line, we might not be lucky enough to get rescued again. There's no reason we shouldn't just sit tight here until the storm lifts and then fly home in the chopper like sensible people."

"Yes, Becky, there's one reason. The *Milk & Honey's* my ship. She's seen me through some hard times and provided my livelihood and yours. And she deserves more than abandonment in the wilderness."

The woman sat on the edge of the desk and ran her fingers through Crick's beard. "Poppa-Bear, I know you love that old clunker. So do I. But it's just a machine, and a burnt-out one at that. Be sensible."

"No. I am going to take my ship home—alone if necessary."

She rose and banged her cocoa cup on the desk top. "All right, be stubborn. Try it if you want. But I won't be a part of it." She stomped out of the room with her back straight and her fists clunched.

Crick knew that she was still upset and frightened by her encounter with Paterson, and that most of her anger at him was further fear of losing him. He knew, too, that when she had time to think it out, she would see through his excuse; she'd been with him too long to believe that even his love of his ship would cloud his judgment on so potentially hazardous an undertaking.

But Becky's faith was not as strong or as clear as his own, and he knew there was no way to explain to her that it wasn't himself, Josiah Crick, who wanted the Honeybucket taken south. Her trust in sanity was fragile just now, and he feared the reaction should he tell her that a Voice had come to him as he knelt by his bunk. And that the Voice had told him that his ancient Mack B-44, known as the *Milk & Honey*, had a part to play in the coming war.

* * * *

Doctor Marvis brought her chunky self into Hardin's office. "Hail, Caesar," she said.

"I don't want to hear it," Hardin replied.

She grunted into a chair and looked sympathetic. "He's that bad, huh?"

"Worse." Hardin rubbed his eyes. "Annie, you wouldn't believe it if I told you."

"Try me."

"Jon came out of that last epilepsis in breakthrough. He woke up perfectly lucid and with a complete, detailed memory of his recurrent dream." He scooted a tape recorder toward himself and turned it on. "Listen to this."

Doctor Marvis listened, her face professionally blank. The tape went on for fifteen minutes before Hardin shut it off.

Marvis gave Hardin a wide-eyed, speculative look. "I have to admit, you don't get one like that every day. Alien races coming to destroy us are common enough, but he's really worked out the details, hasn't he?"

"Yes."

"And I notice his delusion has none of the standard derivative imagery you find in the usual cases. These Lorsii of his sound positively real!"

"That's the problem, Annie. He thinks they are."

"Oh," she said softly. "Oh, dear." She seemed to have trouble with her hands. "I suppose he now thinks he has to rush out and warn the world?"

"I'm afraid so."

Marvis was quiet for a time, blinking rapidly. "He's a good doctor, Lee, and a fine human being. I hope we can do something for him."

Hardin sat up, shaking himself slightly as if to settle himself into a role he did not particularly like. "I am, Annie. I am having him confined as of today." His doctor's face did not quite hide his own pain, and he became brisk to cover it. "Now, what problem did you bring me? Everyone seems to have one today."

She brightened to match his mood, knowing it was as ineffective as his own masquerade. "They're on special today, two for the price of one. First, the Martin woman has asked us to try and dissuade her grandfather from some wild plan he has for salvaging his ship."

Hardin spread his hands. "What can we do? He's a free man and it's his ship. He's not under our jurisdiction except for house rules. If he wants to go out and freeze to death, it's his privilege."

"So I told Miss Martin. But she'd appreciate it if you'd 'try and talk sense' to him."

Hardin looked very tired. "Okay, I'll see what I can do. What next?"

"Zlotny, what else?"

"What's he doing now?"

"Guess who his latest convert is?"

"The Pope?"

"Helva Falstrom."

Hardin's jaw dropped. "The daughter of the President! Good God Almighty."

"That was approximately the reaction the President had, followed almost immediately by a statement to the effect that he was going to cut all the arms and legs off everybody doing research on Zlotny if we don't come up with a sure-fire way to stop our chubby little friend posthaste." She fished a telex tear sheet out of her ample bosom and handed it to Hardin. "WorldGov's brainbank is especially interested in an approach one of our people had— taking Zlotny at face value and attacking him on a religious front. They want we should instanter fly down our boy to consult."

"That figures."

"Nu?"

"The boy in question, Annie dear, is Jon Paterson."

CHAPTER SIX

In the end it was surprisingly easy. Hardin himself gave him the key. "I'm sorry to do this, Jon," he said.

Paterson sat on the floor, against the padded wall, his face perfectly blank.

"It disgusts me to have to put you in the violent ward, but it's all we've got just now. I'll move you to your old quarters as soon as the civilians leave. Meanwhile—" He looked around the bare, ugly room. "If there's anything you want—?"

Paterson stared at the wall. "They're real, Lee. And they're coming. They're going to destroy the earth."

"Yes, well—" Hardin seemed to be leaving everything trailing off. He was having a hard time facing the horrible personification of the fact that illness was bigger than his skill. "Okay, Jon. I've got to run." He stopped in the doorway. "Jon, old friend? Please. Please don't try anything stupid."

Paterson sat crouched against the wall, almost fetal, for a long time after Hardin left. His body was nearly catatonic, but his mind was moving at the speed of light. He knew things now, with a crystalline clarity, and the first of the things he knew was that he had no chance of convincing Lee or anyone else here of the fearsome truth. He knew that the Lorsii were coming, and soon. He knew that the only chance the earth stood, if it had any chance at all, lay in his being able to warn enough people so that some would listen and prepare. And he knew, with a deep cunning, that there was a way to reach the people of the earth. For while no television or radio station would give him access, and no streetcorner preachment would reach enough people, there was Ibrihim Zlotny. He laughed: a harsh, barking sound. There was a poetic justice in the thought that he, a sane man considered crazy, should use the captured broadcast facilities of a crazy man considered sane, to cry forth the real death of the world over that false messiah's own doom prophecies.

There was a lightness about him again, and he saw halos around objects. But this time it wasn't an impending fit. He knew now that his attacks had been caused by his mind's attempts to block out the awfulness of the Lorsii. And he was not blocking that knowledge any more. He had faced it and conquered it. He feared for the earth, and he feared the Lorsii, but he no longer feared his fear. Whatever it was that touched him, that had made him a receptor to the preview of the fall of the Earth, now lifted him in a pillar of fire. A small part of his mind was aware that he was two thousand kilometers from Zlotny, in a frozen, howling wilderness; that he would be hunted and hounded; that every man's hand would be against him. But another part, a deeper, calmer part, knew somehow that he would be guided.

As if detached, as if viewing himself from outside, he got up and walked out of the cell.

* * * *

Rebecca came into the commissary still in her boots and parka, her face raw and red beneath the grease. She went through the line with her tray and received her lunch. Lee Hardin sat alone at a small table in the middle of the room, looking depressed and overworked. Rebecca took her tray over. "Want company?"

Hardin's eyes were grateful. "Yeah." He reached her a chair. "That looks like a touch of frostbite on your nose."

"I'm used to it." They talked of nothing while she ate, but it was a nothing strained at the edges. Finally, she brought up the question. "Have you found him?"

"No, and I'm afraid we won't until spring. It's been three days, now, and he went out in light clothes." Hardin was shaking ever so slightly. "We sent everybody we could spare," he said defensively. "All the patrol service's rescue units, all our own. But what could they expect to find in a blizzard?"

Rebecca shrugged. "What I don't understand is how he did it."

"Sheer stupidity on my part. Jon was a dear personal friend of mine, and I kept forgetting that he was ill. I didn't bother locking the cell door. He apparently figured out that none of the aide staff on the violent ward would know him—he never worked that section—so he just put on a set of whites, picked up a stethoscope and a clipboard, and walked out."

Rebecca could feel Hardin's misery and guilt, and shared it. Intellectually, she knew that she had nothing to do with Paterson's illness, but the memory of her one meeting with him had left her with a nagging suspicion that she had precipitated the crisis which had now resulted in his being frozen to death somewhere out there on the tundra. For a long time, the two people sat together in a cocoon of self-made responsibility.

Hardin cleared his throat. "How are you two coming?"

Rebecca grimaced. "I'm afraid that Grandpa's likely to go through with it. We've managed to wire and hairpin the old rustbucket together, and it looks like his screwy idea will work. I don't know how long the servo motors will take the strain, but they'll actually move the tractor."

"Do you think you'll get your ship back to San Diego?"

"No, but she'll probably make it down to the temperate zone, and I think I can convince the captain that that's good enough. If we can get her as far as the 'States and junk her gracefully, he'll feel that he can visit her. 'Course, he'll never actually do it, but he'll think about it all the time, and that will make him feel good."

Hardin smiled. "You should have been a psychologist, Miss Martin."

"Maybe so." She glanced at her wristwatch. "Well, Poppa-Bear's waiting for his lunch, so I'd better get back out there."

"You'll be leaving us today, then?"

"Tonight sometime. Tires are frozen in, and it'll take three-four more hours for their heating systems to break them loose." She stuck out her hand. "I really want to thank you for your hospitality, Doctor Hardin. We both appreciate it."

"Don't mention it. If you're ever up this way again, stop in and say 'hi.'"

"I'll do that. And if you're ever in San Diego, look us up."

"I will. Drop me a card when you get home, just to let us know you made it."

"Right. Well, bye-bye." She collected a go-tray for her grandfather and left. Hardin watched her retreating back and felt momentarily forlorn that she was not a decade older, or he a decade younger.

* * * *

The rescue unit ground slowly to a halt at the top of a rise, sliding sideways a few meters in the deep, powdery snow until stopped by an enormous, fallen Arctic pine. In the moonlight, her exhausts threw clouds of silver lace into the still air. Inboard, a crewman swung the turret around to face aft and stuck his binoculars against the viewport. Three kilos behind, a single, weak headlamp bounced its beam erratically between the terrain and the star-glittered night sky.

"You got them on visual?"

"Yeah. They're just this side of that last big ravine."

The steersman thumbed his throat mike. "*Milk & Honey*, this is *Grizzly*. Can you still hear us?"

The crewman in the turret squinted into his binoculars. The light far behind blinked once. "He says yes."

"This is as far as we go, Captain Crick. You're eighty clicks nor'-nor'-east of Alberta firebreak sixteen. You should hit it about dawn. Luck to you, sailor; you're on your own." The steersman looked up inquiringly at the man in the turret, who was watching the *Milk & Honey*'s light blink in a series of dots and dashes. "What's he say, Bob?"

"He says, 'Thanks and God bless you.'" The crewman dropped out of the turret and into the copilot's chair. "What d'you think, Boats? Will they make it?"

The steersman threw the unit into gear. "They're rigged like a gypsy circus, a thousand clicks from help, and runnin' so tight on power they won't even use their radio. So what do *you* think?"

"I think we'd better finish our patrol and get some sleep. We'll have to come dig out the remains in a couple of days."

The *Grizzly* thundered to life and spun on her long axis, easing off down the rise. She climbed over the fallen pine, dislodging it and sending it rolling down the rise in a miniature avalanche of powder and ice. And then she was gone.

The pine had left a frozen windbreak behind it, an almost-cave in the slope. Something stirred in the scoop of protection. Something shaggy and rimed. It rose, staggering upright—slipped, rolled down the rise, rose again. Alone on the cold, moonlit plain, it lurched in a circle. It stopped, facing north toward the *Milk & Honey*'s bobbing yellow light. As if attracted, it began half-walking, half-falling.

Rebecca saw it first and screamed. She climbed over the back of her chair, her eyes wide. "Grandpa! What *is* that thing?"

Crick pushed the makeshift rheostat to neutral and the servos whined to a stop, leaving the tractor in eerie silence. He put a finger behind his glasses and pushed them out to the end of his nose, then wiped the frost off the inside of the windshield. There was a strange exultation on his face. "That, Becky, is a man who is wrapped in chunks of moss and covered with ice and snow." He smiled in satisfaction. "Should've known he'd think of something like that. One of the crewmen on the *Freuken* walked out of Amundsonland that way, back in—"

"Poppa-Bear, you don't suppose that's—?"

"Who else?" Crick said, reaching for his gloves. "Can't be that many folks strolling around out here at eighteen below. Let's get him inside."

They carried Paterson in, Crick pushing from below and Rebecca hauling from above. He was semiconscious and unable to offer any help. They could not get him up into a bunk and laid him out on the deckplates between the control chairs.

"My Lord," Rebecca said in disbelief. "Look at him, Grandpa. I think his hand's frozen solid. I'm afraid to touch it for fear I'll snap his fingers off."

"Get some cold water, child. Then some warm soup. Warm, mind you, not hot."

Rebecca ran for the galley, then ran back. "Get on the radio. We'll have to call the *Grizzly*. They'll get him to the hospital."

"No. Get the water."

Rebecca stood still. "What do you mean, 'no?' Grandpa, this guy's dying! It's a miracle he's not dead already."

Crick looked up. "Yes, it is," he said in complete seriousness.

Rebecca Martin looked down at her grandfather as though seeing him for the first time; as though he were a stranger suddenly come into her life around a corner. "Josiah," she said, speaking in an odd voice, "are you going to let him die?"

"No. He'll not die. The Lord brought him to us to help in our work."

Rebecca felt as if she were going to break into small, sharp pieces. "You're not going to San Diego, are you? You're going after Zlotny."

"As God wills."

Paterson shuddered violently. Croaking sounds came from his throat. He clutched at Crick, who was bent over him, and levered himself to a sitting psition. His bloodshot, ice-burned eyes drilled like bullets into the old man's face. "Zlotny," he rasped. "Zlotny!"

Crick turned a triumphant face to his granddaughter. "You see? Do you realize now what Ibrihim Zlotny is child?"

She just stared, mute, her eyes filling with tears.

"Zlotny," Crick said, speaking as though to someone very young, "is the Antichrist."

CHAPTER SEVEN

President Falstrom strode painfully through the throng of reporters, working to see that his limp didn't show. He kept a jovial and slightly distant look on his ruddy features and fielded the newsmongers' hammer of questions with professional noncommitment.

"Mister President," a bespectacled man asked, "what is WorldGov's position on the use of force?"

"You'd have to ask the Secretary for Military Affairs that question," Falstrom answered, easing toward his door. "You know that such decisions are her province."

A woman stepped in front of Falstrom, cutting him off. "Mister President, is there any truth to the rumor that your daughter gave Zlotny's people secret documents detailing the placement of WorldGov's atomic installations?"

There was a murmur of embarrassment from the other reporters, and Falstrom's face tightened, but the woman stood her ground.

The President shook his head ever so slightly. "No, Ms. Rodgers, there is no truth to that rumor. Helva simply...left us."

"It *is* true that she went willingly, isn't it?"

"Yes, that part is true."

"What are you doing about it?"

Falstrom reached around the woman and got his hand on the doorknob. "Do you have children?"

"Two."

"Have you seen them since this morning?"

The reporter opened her mouth, but nothing came out. A brief fear flickered in her face, and she dropped her eyes. "I'm sorry, Mister President. Thank you."

Falstrom let himself into his office and closed the door just a little too hard. His secretary came forward with two aspirin and a glass of milk, and he accepted them gratefully. "Maggie, get the Turkish Secretary here as soon as possible. And the American, also." He went to his private office and took his aspirin, staring out through his bulletproof picture window at the Hague, still beautiful after all these centuries, still unaffected by sixty years of being the seat of world government. But Falstrom's mind was not on the lovely old city. He pounded the window sill with his fist. "Damn Zlotny to hell!"

He was more composed ten minutes later when a young, dark woman entered, followed by a squat man with enormous moustaches. "Hello, Charlotte; hello, Armin. Sit down." He began to pace the room, his limp showing now. "I'll get right to it. We've got to do something about Zlotny, and now. Another week of his blackmail and the whole world's going to panic."

"Half of it already has," Charlotte said. "Chicago and San Francisco are nearly ghost towns, with everybody trying to get out before Zlotny's bomb squad gets itchy-fingered. Dallas is on fire and the police estimate there are over ten thousand people doing nothing but looting full time. The zombies have completely taken over Chattanooga and Atlanta."

The Turk's face showed equal gloom. "The secretariat says that the whole Bosphorus Crescent is 'out of contact,' Lars. Best I can figure it, that means Zlotny's people have complete control of the communications and transport facilities." He tugged the corners of his moustache nervously. "Wish I could tell you something hopeful."

The President grimaced. "The worst part is that we can no longer trust our information. Director Elston told me in confidence this morning that he thinks better than half his own agents are working for Zlotny. Every single man he's sent in to infiltrate the outfit has turned into a Zlotny fanatic—. How the *hell* are we supposed to function when our own intelligence system is riddled with enemies?"

The American Secretary was watching Falstrom closely. "Lars, if I recognize the signs correctly, you've got something up your sleeve."

Falstrom acknowledged her insight. "But it's a desperation measure, and if it doesn't work we'll all go down in flames." He went to his desk and pressed a switch. The room filled with the peculiar underwater sensation of scrambled air. Falstrom came over and sat on the arm of the Turkish Secretary's chair. "Armin, Charlotte, there's one small piece of data we've managed to secure. It was just part of a mass of trivia until a doctor up in Canada noticed it and its possible importance."

Armin looked hopeful.

Falstrom leaned over conspiratorially. "There are no insane people among Zlotny's followers."

The Turk's hopeful look changed to disappointment. "Damn, Lars, the whole lot of them are crazy."

"No, what I mean is that neither he nor his followers have managed to convert anyone with mental problems."

Charlotte saw it first. "And that means we have an immune group to work with!"

"Exactly. So what we have to do is find a mental case who can be persuaded or coerced into—removing Ibrihim Zlotny."

Armin made a growling sound. "Lars—Mister President—I don't think that's a good idea. If we take Zlotny out, we'll have two million fanatics going into a holy war, not to mention two dozen of them pushing buttons and blowing a billion people into radioactive cinders."

The American's face was tense with concentration. She shook her head and laid her hand on her fellow Secretary's arm. "Wait a minute, Armin, I think I see where Lars is going." She turned to the President. "We take Zlotny out, preferably with someone who stands for all he's against, and we're ready with a blitz on the com circuits designed to put the zombies in doubt— the glorious leader getting offed and all that."

The Turkish Secretary saw it. "Right! That might give us the couple hours we need for a commando against the bomb emplacements."

Falstrom smiled in satisfaction. "We know where all the bombs are. It's just a question of getting a man to the triggermen before they can drop the deadman switches. If we can confuse them for five minutes, we can get them."

Enthused now, the Turk stood up. "Where do we start, Lars?"

Falstrom pointed to a world map which covered one wall of the office. "Somewhere out there is a lunatic who wants to kill Ibrihim Zlotny, or who can be convinced that he does. Go find him. I've enough trustworthy people left to assure that he gets near Zlotny."

"Near isn't good enough, Lars."

Falstrom's smile was both genuine and malicious. "I'm told

that the insane often succeed where others fail because they do not think in normal patterns. Let's be sure our man is both subtle and cunning, and let him find his own path into Zlotny's maze."

The two General Secretaries made their departure, each already deep into the plan. Falstrom sat on the chair arm after they left, brooding. He wished that he could be as confident of his brainstorm as his subordinates were. But he could not quite believe that the salvation of the world, and of his beloved, sweet, harmless daughter Helva, lay in the hands of an as-yet-unfound madman.

* * * *

The two boys stood on the littered street corner, watching looters ransack a burning building across the street. They were scruffy, nervous, and about fourteen.

"Man," said the first, "lookit them stereos. Wish I had one."

The second glanced up and down the street furtively. "Why'n't we go get one? Everybody else is."

"Naw. The cops'll be along in a minute and put stunstiks on them guys."

"Not a chance. Th' Army's got this whole block under control." The way he said "army" left no doubt that it was the Army of the Final Testament he meant, rather than WorldGov's troops.

The first boy kicked a can into the gutter, his hands fidgeting with his belt. "Naw. Those guys're too weird for me. I don't trust 'em."

A deeper voice spoke from behind them. "A worthy attitude, sinner. It will serve you well."

Both boys jumped and turned. A tough-looking man in his twenties stood smiling at them, his jackbooted feet planted wide and his gloved hands holding a silver stunstik across his thighs. His skull was shaved except for pomaded horns at each temple. The burning building cast a flickering, blood-red light on his face. "Trust only in your own judgment, young sinner, and in your common sense. The Duality has no need of people who cannot think."

The nervous boy backed up a step or two, but the other one stood still, open admiration on his face. He self-consciously made the curious salute of Zlotny's army—the left hand raised with thumb and middle two fingers folded, forming the ancient sign of the evil eye; the right hand with index finger athwart the index of the left, making a parody of a cross. "Nema," he said loudly.

The trooper looked from one to the other, grinning slyly. "You were watching those sinners yonder, yes? You were envying them the riches they are acquiring." He took several swift steps along the wall of the nearest building, which housed a jewelry store, and laid his stunstik against the glass of the display window, all the while watching the two boys with his sly grin. He raised his eyebrows as if asking permission, then with a single, savage motion, smashed the glass with the stunstik. Using the tip of the stick, he fished out a strand of diamonds and flicked it casually toward the boys. The second kid caught it, his eyes wide and mouth agape. The trooper walked back over to them. "Riches? Women? Power? What are these? They are yours, young sinners, for the asking. You do not have to believe in the Duality to get them: we give them to you freely. And why?"

Both boys shook their heads to indicate noncomprehension.

"Because beside *our* wealth and power, these things are as clay and rubbish." His smile widened as he saw comprehension dawn in the youngsters' faces. "Now," he said softly, "who will come with me? Who will pick up the staff of the Servant? Who will stand with him in the final days?"

The second boy stepped forward as if in a trance, his face radiant. "I will. Yeah, man, take me!"

The nervous boy looked as though he wanted to say something to his friend, but did not. He just stepped back a few steps, then turned and ran.

The trooper quietly pressed a button on the small com unit he wore on his belt and started walking the eager youth up the street, his arm around the child's shoulders in a comradely fashion. As they came to an intersection, an intracity truck rolled up. A smear of white paint covered the merchant's name on its flanks, and Zlotny's lightning-slashed and horned cross was stenciled over it.

The trooper led the youth behind the truck and faced him toward it, then stepped unobtrusively back. A loudspeaker mounted atop the vehicle blared forth the seductive, martial anthem of the Army of the Final Testament, and the rear doors swung open. Inside, red light played on a heavy oak altar with a holo projection of a moody, storm-lashed sky behind it. On either side of the altar stood two beautiful young girls, naked to the waist. They smiled and beckoned. A ramp slid silently down from the tailgate. His eyes riveted on the swaying breasts of the girls, the boy marched up into the truck. The ramp slid up, the doors closed, and the truck pulled away.

The trooper's smile was gone. His face became wooden, his eyes vacant. Not the face of a man who had lost control, it was the slack, formless face of the mindless. It was the face of a man who was controlled, but by someone or something else.

He thumbed the com unit and spoke in a voice devoid of emotion or overtone. "Delivered one, lost one. Coordinates fiver, fiver, three, south; fiver, niner, zero, west. Suggest pursuit and destruction of negative sinner."

The com unit grated metallically. "Negative pursuit and destruction. Proceed coordinates four, six, niner, south; zero, zero, eight, east. Female sinner plus or minus three years alone in building. Receiver unit will meet you there in ten minutes."

"Affirmative." The trooper turned and strode off, his sly grin returning as he passed a knot of teenaged looters. He saluted them with his silver stunstik. "All things are possible through the Duality, young sinners. All things are permissible."

* * * *

The *Milk & Honey* mushed south through driving curtains of rain, the ground beneath her three-meter-high tires so soggy it was impossible to tell if she was fording streams or running on tundra. Rebecca Martin was at the helm, swinging the big steering wheel in quick arcs, her foot jamming the accelerator—now rigged to an electrical rheostat—to the deckplates. Even with all her concentration centered on the slewing tractor and the slurred landscape outside, a part of her kept her back rigidly and somehow defiantly arched, her chin at a disdainful attitude. She had created an invisible but very definite wall of ice between herself and the two men who sat casually anchored to the galley table's handholds, their coffee mugs swinging in their gymbaled, magnetic bases.

To all appearances, Rebecca's attitude, and indeed, even her existence, was unnoticed by her grandfather and Paterson, whose intense expressions belied the relaxed postures they affected. They had been arguing quietly for the better part of three hours, and neither seemed inclined to stop now.

"Tell me again what they look like, Doctor," Crick said mildly.

Paterson picked up his coffee cup awkwardly: his hands were heavily bandaged. He blew on the cup, though the liquid in it was long since cold. "In a weird way, they look human. I mean, they've got two arms and two legs, and—"

"In that computer enhancement I found on your desk, they had four arms."

"Yeah, but I wasn't seeing them as clearly then. I think maybe they have two sets of wings. The big batlike ones and maybe something firmer, more chitinous. Like beetles or something." He grimaced and shook his head. "Or maybe not. They're still not all that clear."

Crick brushed his flowing beard with his fingers. "You know, I 'member seeing holos of medieval demons that looked a lot like your Lorsii."

Paterson snorted. "Don't you think I thought of that? Hell, everybody's seen gargoyles sometime or other. But I'm not projecting fantasy memories or Breughel's paintings."

"Not what I was getting at, son. There's a difference between gargoyles and demons. You ever read descriptions of demons—real ones, Satan's servants?"

Paterson sighed. "Look, old man, you've got the right to your beliefs. But don't try and push them off on me; I've been through it. My father was a lay preacher. I've heard all that stuff I ever want to hear—twice."

"Yep, I guess you have. Of course, that don't make them any less real—the demons, I mean. None of us like to be reminded of the ugly parts of life, but they're still there."

Paterson fumbled a cigarette out of his pocket, annoyed that he was chain-smoking but unable to do anything about it. "Why is it, Captain, that you can sit there and argue the existence of demons and witches—"

"Just demons, son."

"—and expect me to take them seriously, while you yourself utterly refuse to consider the Lorsii as real? Do you know how good the odds are on there being other life in the universe?"

" 'Bout a million to one in favor, if I remember."

"About a mill—" Paterson shook his head. "And you still refuse to believe in them?"

"No," Crick said softly. "It's just definitions we differ on. You ever consider that we might look like demons to another race? Or that God in His wisdom might have implanted that race with an image of their particular curse, even though that curse might come from across the galaxy?"

Paterson opened his mouth, frowned, and shut it again. He listened intently, though his face was set in stubborn lines.

"Now who's to say," Crick argued, "that with all the universe to use as He sees fit, God doesn't bring each of us the Story in the way we can best use it?"

"I don't see what you're getting at, Crick."

"Well, what makes you think He hasn't sent his Son to all the sentient races the same way he did here—as one of their own?"

"You mean, a race of bugs would have a bug Jesus?"

"I mean a race that thinks and feels would have the knowledge

58

of good and evil given it in its own terms." Crick leaned forward on his elbows. "And maybe the angels and demons those folks have are weird creatures with fur on their chins and five fingers on their hands and bloodshot eyes, eh?"

Paterson looked as if the idea were repugnant. "I can't see me as anybody's demon, Crick. I don't go around tormenting people."

"Ever swat a fly? Step on a bug? Eat a slab of butchered cow?"

"Those things don't think, Crick."

"You mean that they don't think in any ways you and me can recognize."

"You're playing semantic games, old man."

"You're avoiding the obvious, Doctor. You're so determined to see these Lorsii of yours as an alien menace, you can't admit that they might be that *and* God's demons, too. You're doing what the skeptic always does: making labored, awkward assumptions to avoid simple truths. The fact is that since God created all of us— including the Lorsii—He uses all of us."

Paterson grunted and lay back in his chair, weary and in pain. "Look, old man, you go attack Ibrihim Zlotny if you want. You argue him blue and fight your own Armageddon and believe what you want. But none of that will change the fact that the Lorsii are coming and coming fast. And I've got to warn the world."

Rebecca Martin cut into the conversation with a single, terse word: "Border."

Crick and Paterson looked up. "Bravo, child," the Captain said. "Whereabouts?"

"I haven't had time to check the 'finder," she snaped. "I'm having enough trouble just keeping us right side up."

Crick levered himself out of the galley chair and came to the console, moving easily with the lurch and roll of the 'liner. "Well, now," he said jovially, "let's just take a fix and find out what part of God's real estate we're on." He slipped into a set of headphones and began tuning the directional antenna atop the cabin, seeking the coded radio signals broadcast by position towers in the vicinity. "Mmmm."

Crick switched the ranging radio off. "I make us fourteen klicks over the border, 'bout sixty klicks nor'-west of Bismarck. Should hit U.S. Freightway eighty shortly." He turned to Paterson. "Ever been on a freightway, son? These 'liners're too big for highways, so they got roads of their own, runnin' between all the major terminals. Actually just big swatches o'land where the hills have been knocked down and the trees cleared out some. But a darn sight smoother than open country. You wouldn't know it by lookin', but some of these big ships can really roll when you give 'em room. The old *New Orleans* could put fifty kilotons on her back and run at forty knots. An' I remember back when I was a wiper on the *Sandra D. Trahan*—"

Rebecca took her foot off the pedal and the Honeybucket whined to a stop. Rain thundered on the metal roof and bulkheads of the cabin, and lightning flashes lit her face. She stood up.

"What's wrong, child? Why are you stopping?"

She walked the tilted deck to the galley and pulled a cup of coffee out of the percolator, then took it to the galley table. "Come sit down, Josiah." She dropped into a chair opposite Paterson, glaring at him with unmitigated dislike.

Crick came over and sat, his face showing that he had an idea of what she was about to say.

She lit herself a cigarette, paused, then lit one for Paterson, sticking it between his lips with no sign of friendship. "I think it's time we faced a few things, Josiah, and this is as good a place to do it as any."

"All right, Becky. What do you think needs facing?" Crick tossed a quick look at Paterson, but found him staring into his cup.

"First off," she said, holding up one finger as though explaining things to a child, "we are back in the 'States. A border patrolman is going to show up sooner or later—probably sooner—and want to see our manifests. What do you intend to tell him when he asks for this, this—person's papers?"

Crick's look was bland. "Why, that he lost them in his accident."

Rebecca sighed. "Don't be stupid, Poppa-Bear. They'd impound us. Look, Mister Paterson is a sick man, any way you want to consider it. He's also an escaped mental case, and if we are caught with him aboard we'll go to jail."

"Now, Becky, I don't think it's all—"

"Second, the servo motors were never meant to drive a tractor and they're just waiting around to burn out. They're not going to last long enough to get us where you want to go." She said the last with pointed emphasis.

"Possibly, but—"

"Third, I'm not going to let you try it." The finality of her statement was unmistakable.

Crick looked indignant. "Rebecca Martin! This is my ship. I own it and I command it. I will take it where I wish and the Lord wills."

"Not by yourself." She dropped her eyes, unable to face the hurt and disbelief in her grandfather's face. "I'm sorry, Poppa-Bear. I can't let you try this. It's a fool's errand. You're too old, and you're a-all I've got." She was near tears.

Crick reached out for her but didn't quite touch her. "Becky," he said, his own voice quavering. "Becky, it's not yours to decide, or even mine. It's the Lord's will. I've told you that. Ibrihim Zlotny is the enemy of God, and I have been called to stop him."

The girl leapt up, her face twisted. "Called! So's Zlotny been 'called'—according to him. So's Jon, here—according to him! I think you're *all* nuts." She took a shaky breath and sat back down. "I'm sorry, Grandpa. I didn't mean that."

"Yes, you did. And that's natural. It is a frightening thing to be touched by the finger of God. More frightening to those who love you and have not been touched. Mister Paterson and I share a thing with the false prophet, child. We are all thought crazy by those around us. But there is a real difference between Zlotny and us here. Mister Paterson and I are harming no one, while that son of Satan is bringing great evil into the world." He leaned forward, his glasses sliding down his nose. "Surely that is sufficient reason to oppose him, Becky, even if it were not a command from God?"

"Yes, it is," she agreed. "But not for a seventy-two-year-old man and a guy who thinks bugs from outer space are about to come and eat us all up. WorldGov's not just standing around. They'll find a way to stop Zlotny."

"They haven't thus far, child."

"That's irrelevant. The point is, Poppa-Bear, that *you* can't stop him."

"Even if the Lord says I can?" He said it softly.

Rebecca Martin spun her cup between her palms and spoke, obviously picking her words carefully. "Grandpa, I am a Christian, too. You've raised me to be a good one, and I think I am. I have been a dutiful granddaughter to you. I am chaste and moral, and charitable to the less fortunate. I know that I am proud and not forgiving of my enemies, but I believe God understands my imperfection." She looked her grandfather in the eye. "I've prayed, Poppa-Bear. For guidance and understanding. And you know what? I still can't believe that God wants you to throw away your long and good life on some hare-brained scheme to do away with Ibrihim Zlotny."

"The Lord moves in mysterious ways, His wonders to perform."

Rebecca saw that she wasn't going to change his mind. She stood up and pointed. "All right. But the Honeybucket moves *that* way, to Bismarck. I'm going to put her in United Fruit's terminal and let the bureaucrats sort out what to do with her and our flippo friend here."

Paterson's silence through the debate had caused him to fade into the background. Rebecca Martin's comment brought attention back to him, and he looked at the girl with a strange face. "No, Miss Martin, you're not. You're going to do whatever your conscience dictates—with yourself. But this ship goes south, along with

Captain Crick and me."

"Just who the hell do you think you are, mister?"

"Don't swear, child," Crick admonished.

Rebecca ignored him, her face red and her eyes flashing. "You've got no say in this, Paterson. You'd be dead if we hadn't hauled you out of the ice. You owe us your life, and we don't owe you a damn thing."

"Don't swea—"

"Do you think you can pirate this ship, buddy? If so, I've got news for you. I've been on 'liners since I was seventeen, and there's no two-bit bully-boy alive I can't take bare-handed. You want to try a takeover, you just make your move. I'll show you tricks you didn't know existed. I'll—"

"Sit down." Paterson's voice cut like a whip, and Rebecca sat down before she knew she'd done it. Surprise overlaid the anger in her features. Surprise and perhaps a little fear. Paterson stuck his now-dead cigarette out, and she removed it from between his lips almost as if compelled. "Miss Martin," Paterson said calmly. "Rebecca. It is the captain's decision, not mine. And not yours, either. He is going after Zlotny, and I am going with him. You can come along, or stay, as you wish. But that's the way it is."

Rebecca looked to her grandfather, her eyes pleading. He nodded affirmation. "It's the Lord's will, Becky."

She got up, her hands resting lightly on the galley table. Her smile was bitter. "All right. I seem to be outvoted."

"You'll stay with us, Becky?"

"You'll need a copilot. And I can't leave the Honeybucket in the hands of two fruitcakes." She marched to the pilot's chair and threw herself into it. It was still a long way to Colorado, and there would be time to plan. Time to find a way to stop this madness. She floored the pedal and the Honeybucket sloshed off through the mud and rain...headed south.

CHAPTER EIGHT

Ibrihim Zlotny sat back in his seat and peered out the small window in the chopper's hull. A hundred meters away, another chopper hung in the air protectively, lasercannon bristling from its gunbays. Zlotny knew there were six just like it forming an aerial sphere with himself at the center, and that farther out, on the horizon, a larger sphere of planes, 'copters and missiles cocooned him. And farther still, in silos buried in the desert, on crags in the sides of mountains, interceptors recently manned by WorldGov troops now stood ready at the command of the Army of the Final Testament to stop ICBMs at the edges of the continent. No leader in history, Zlotny knew, had ever been so guarded.

But these things were on the periphery of the moon-faced man's mind. The center of his concentration lay a thousand meters below, where the grassy sea of the Oklahoma plain writhed with a multicolored sargassum of humanity. It stretched for seven kilometers in every direction, and Zlotny mentally computed it at close to three million souls.

Even as he watched, the pointillist dot-work of color shifted to a uniform pinkish tan as three million faces lifted to the sound and sight of his coming. A physical wave of sound beat skyward, audible even over the thrum of the chopper.

An aide appeared at Zlotny's side, smiling. "This will be the greatest conversion of all time, Master. We have every portable altar in North America down there, and some we've brought in from India and the Chinese hegemony."

Zlotny's baby-face creased into pleasure wrinkles. "And do you think I will disappoint them, fellow servant?"

The boy's face registered shock and horror. "No! What the Master promises, the Master delivers."

"By the grace of the Duality, my son. I am but another servant, even as you are."

The boy's look changed to pride and trust. "It is thus written, Servant Zlotny." He said the last slowly, as if sharing something precious, the line connecting his servitude and Zlotny's clearly valuable to him.

The chopper landed in a cleared space in the midst of the enormous crowd. Zlotny stepped out to a cheer which shook the ground and mounted an aluminum stepset to a platform high over the gathering. Behind and above him, a huge television screen magnified his image and broadcast it over the massed people. Several other screens repeated the image at half-kilometer distances radiating outward from the platform. Zlotny raised his hands in the salute of the Army of the Final Testament. "Greetings, sinners. I am Ibrihim Zlotny." The answering roar went on for a long time.

Zlotny spoke for an hour, delivering his message and calling witnesses to the platform to testify to the miracles which had been wrought by the Duality. Here a man who had been cured of disease; there a girl who had been lifted from the darkness of retardation into the light of intelligence. And as the exhortations and testimonies went on, Zlotny eyed the gathering with more intensity than his face displayed, for this group was not as homogeneous as it seemed. Closest to the platform were the true believers, those who had come knowing they would enter the altar trucks. They formed a ring a kilometer deep. Behind them were the skeptics, the curious, the "maybe" set. And behind them were the professional hangers-on who coalesced around any crowd. At the outer fringes were the fearful parents and friends, searching for the lost son or daughter or brother, hoping to save the loved one from Zlotny's blandishments.

And scattered through the whole mass were people with more deadly concerns. A hundred thousand strong, the Army of the Final Testament's soldiers circulated quietly, some in uniform, some in mufti. Their eyes were hard and never still, and their hands never far from stunstik or lasergun. For osmoting though the fervent mass of humanity with them were the agents of WorldGov, themselves possibly numbering in the thousands: men and women, boys and girls, even children; each here to gather information, to sabotage, and possibly to strike at the Great Servant himself. Less numerous but equally deadly were the free agents—Christian zealots, thrill

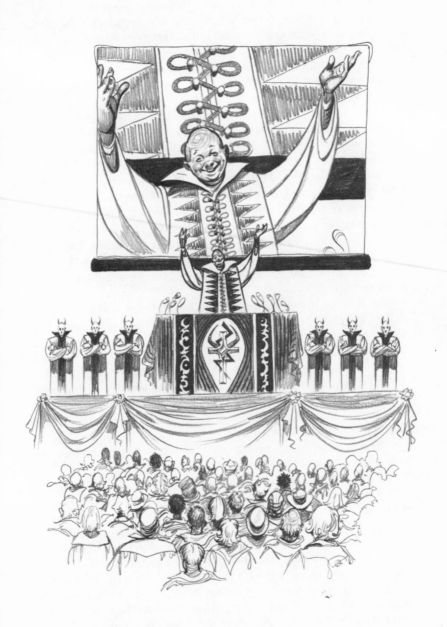

seekers, headline hounds, and people with a simple taste for murder. A war was in progress in the crowd, although it made not a sound and caused not a ripple. A WorldGov agent was found trying to get a camera into an altar truck and died with his finger on the shutter. A woman swollen in pregnancy was snatched as she made her way toward the platform, a soldier strangling her as two others defused the bomb strapped to her stomach. A man on top of a homemade ladder four kilometers from the platform got a beam of coherent green light through the back of his skull even as he sighted Zlotny through his high-power rifle's scope.

Nor was it one-sided. Here and there knots of curious people gathered around a soldier who lay prostrate with heat or excitement—induced by fatal overdoses of various drugs. And back in the hectare-square parking area, seveal innocent-looking trucks and vans were slowly filling up with Zlotnyites, bound and gagged.

The sun began to set and the people grew restless. Zlotny had promised a miracle, and this is what they had come to see. Thus far, nothing had been seen but the standard preachment of the Duality. The more experienced among the audience recognized the delay as showmanship.

But at last the recitations ended, the harangue was concluded. Zlotny's magnified image beamed out over the multitude. "My friends, sinners and faithful," he said, "it is the appointed time. I have promised you an irrefutable proof of the power of the Left Hand, and I will now give it to you."

The crowd fell silent. Zlotny pointed to the western sky, toward a bright glitter just above the sinking sun. "Behold in the heavens, my friends. There in the coldness of the void hangs a dead rock. It is called by scientists 'the visitor.' "

Three million faces swung west, as many hands shielding as many pairs of eyes.

In a high, penetrating voice, Zlotny cried out. "Look upon the wonder in the heavens, sinners, and know joy. The Left Hand is among us!"

The glittering dot above the sun suddenly blossomed, its glare so intense that Sol itself was eclipsed. A chorus of cries, shouts, and shrieks went up from the millions on the plain and was followed immediately by an even greater acclamation. The incandescent ball of light was spreading, separating before their very eyes into smaller pinpricks of violent illumination. Even as they watched, the lights began to form a design. And the design was apparent to eyes prepared and conditioned: a horned cross was appearing in the heavens.

Zlotny was off the platform, walking toward an armored van in a ring of muscular guards. Hordes of believers fell to their knees or prostrated themselves as he passed. On the platform, a senior sergeant was exhorting the people to step forward, to enter the altar trucks whose rear doors were now open and whose ramps were down. The mass of people began to thicken in places, thin in others. By dark it had shaped itself into a dozen lines, some a hundred souls wide and a hundred thousand long. They marched into the rear of the trucks with fear and worship and joy on their faces, and they marched out the front with uniformly wonderstruck commitment displayed, to be formed into groups of thirteen and multiples of thirteen and marched away into the darkness by soldiers of the Army.

Zlotny sat in his armored van, watching the procession through a bulletproof window and smiling quietly. Aides came and went with tabulations and logistics problems.

A colonel, barely twenty, bent near Zlotny's ear. "Is the Great Servant ready to rest?"

Zlotny considered, then nodded. "Yes, I think I will. It seems that the conversion goes smoothly."

"It does, Master."

"We have sufficient receivers, sufficient serum?"

"Yes, Master. I have assured that."

"Then I shall retire." He rose and peered through the window to the floodlit altar truck nearby.

The colonel followed his gaze. "Does the Servant wish, ah, a companion?"

Zlotny nodded, his smile bland and innocent. "Yes. I believe that young sinner in the yellow jumper is worthy of personal guidance as she comes into the fold." He indicated a child of ten or eleven.

"Shall I bring her before she's been through the truck, Master?"

"Oh, yes," Zlotny answered softly. "She will be much more...spirited that way."

And overhead, the remnants of the meteoroid called "the visitor" continued to fly apart, and the horned cross of the Duality arched over the plains of Oklahoma in malevolent fire.

* * * *

President Falstrom flicked the ball-bearing with his finger, watching in deep concentration as it rolled noisily down the ninemeter length of the highly polished table. In the cavernous conference room, the sound was disproportionately loud and disproportionately ugly.

The ball-bearing reached the end of the table and was stopped by Charlotte Honesdale's dark hand. She picked it up, marble style, and propelled it back up the table. The two statespersons had been rolling the bearing for half an hour.

"The worst part," the American Secretary said, "isn't his parlor trick with that meteoroid, but the way he suborned the agents. We had two hundred people assigned to play converts and get inside those damned trucks of his. They all made it, and they all came out the other end as rabid Zlotnyites."

"And the first thing they did," Falstrom said disgustedly, "was point out the rest of the agents. I think we lost over nine thousand of our best people in that mess." He stopped the ball-bearing and toyed with it. "The part I don't understand is how he could have gotten to so many *kinds* of agents. We had people under drugs, hypnoed people, fanatics, handkillers, people wired to explode."

"And they all failed."

"And they all failed."

Charlotte sat up. "Speaking of fanatics, did any of those people score? I mean, the civilians?"

"Nowhere that counted. We kept tabs on about fifty religious nuts and gun freaks, and all of them got scotched by the zombies. A couple got close, though. One got within about ninety meters of Zlotny himself before they killed him." Falstrom looked thoughtful. "Come to think of it, they got closer than anyone else."

"Any of them certifiable mental cases?"

"I don't think so. At least, none that we were watching. You still think that's our best bet?"

She tapped the stack of reports beside her elbow with a long fingernail. "The score's still perfect. Not one real nut's ever been converted." She pulled a report and flipped it open. "Right now, we've got about a dozen people we're watching who may have a chance at getting Zlotny. The most promising, I think, are a woman from Germany who thinks Zlotny is her dead husband come back, and a freightliner captain who's a devout Baptist and thinks Zlotny is the Antichrist. The German woman was doing fifteen-to-life in Munich for murdering her husband, and has managed to escape and elude all authorities. She's gotten as far as, ah—" Charlotte consulted the folder. "Miami. Our people down there believe she might get through."

"And the freighterman?"

"Elmer Josiah Crick. He's one of those ingenious old fellows who can find a way to do anything. He's been running his 'liner on prayers and chewing gum for seven or eight years now." She cocked her head and frowned. "I'll be damned. Lars, the old man's apparently got with him an escapee from the Alberta poke-and-probe hospital, and guess who it is?"

"I give up."

"Doctor Jon Paterson. Ring a bell?"

"Not offhand."

"He's the man who originated the idea of sending a religious nut after Zlotny. Seems he was more a patient than a staff member up there. They had him in for nightmares, which it turns out he believes are real. Something about an alien race invading the earth."

President Falstrom shook his head. "Maybe that's what we need. It's put a stop to Zlotny." He tossed the ball-bearing back down the table again. "Well, let's see if we can ease their paths, at least as far as we've still got control. Maybe one of the bunch will get a shot at our friendly neighborhood messiah."

"Self-styled, that is."

"And so far, successful; blast his cherubic face and soul to hell."

"Amen."

* * * *

Hezekiah stalked halfheartedly across the enormous tire, while Beelzebub scurried disinterestedly just ahead of him. On the one occasion, several months previous, when the cat had actually caught the mouse, both animals had been so startled that neither could face the other for several days. Thereafter, both had taken care not to cause a repeat of the embarrassing incident.

Just above them, Paterson and Rebecca Martin sat on the 'liner's fender. Captain Crick leaned out of the hatch just behind them. All three stared in grim silence to the southeast, where the twilight sky glowed a sinister red. An hour earlier they had rolled the *Milk & Honey* through the smoking and corpse-littered remains of Prescott, Arizona, where they had found the pastor of the Methodist church crucified to the front of his building with ten-penny nails. Now they sat on the rim of the mesa which held Prescott and watched as Phoenix, three kilometers below and ninety away, smeared the horizon crimson in its death agonies.

"It's horrible," Rebecca said.

"It's Armageddon, child," Crick replied.

"It doesn't matter," Paterson said, levering himself off the fender. "Let's get going."

Rebecca bared her teeth. "Listen to him, Grandpa! Millions of people dying down there and he says it doesn't matter! This is the guy you pulled out of the snow! This is the man you're taking with you! Are you sure you're after the right spawn of Satan?"

Paterson stopped with one bandaged hand on the hatch and

69

regarded Rebecca Martin levelly. "Most of the people down there aren't dying. They're either rioting or drunk or fornicating. They're part of Zlotny's army now, and everything is permissible. After all, they've got proof that their leader has the inside track." He pointed with his chin to the horned cross hanging in the sky, now three days old and covering a large quadrant of the firmament.

"Bull! There's a hundred ways he could have rigged that."

"Name one. Better yet, convince one of the good citizens of Phoenix, down there—that is, if you can get them to stop stealing and burning long enough to listen."

Rebecca turned her back on him, furious but unable to retort.

Paterson slid into the cabin and waited for Captain Crick to join him.

The old man came in and took the command chair, but did not put the 'liner in motion. He pulled his Bible from beneath the dashboard and opened it. "Jon, you ever read the Word?"

"No. Well, when I was a kid. My father was religious."

"Ever read the Old Testament?"

"No."

Crick thumbed the worn book's pages as though caressing an old friend. "There was the prophet Ezekiel, Jon, remember him?"

"What is this, Crick? Twenty questions?"

"Ezekiel."

"No."

"Okay. Let's say you—Jon Paterson—are standing among the exiles on the banks of the Chebar River, over in Chaldea, a few thousand years ago. Let's say you've come as a psychologist to interview a preacher name of Ezekiel."

Rebecca had come in, and both she and Paterson were watching Crick with a mixture of curiosity and impatience. "Okay," Paterson said. "Let's suppose it."

"Let's say that while you're fussing with your wire recorders and cameras, and he's consulting his scrolls, something happens."

"Like what?"

"Well, that's what I'm coming to. Let's say that Brother Ezekiel sees this thing happen, and so do you, and then you go your separate ways. You get into your time machine and come back here, and Ezekiel goes running off to the temple. Now, he collars his fellow preachers and says, 'Guess what! I've just been visited by angels of the Lord.'" Crick smiled at his granddaughter and the hardfaced Paterson. "And what happens?"

"They laugh at him," Paterson replied.

"Not quite. They say, 'Oh, yeah? What did they look like?' And Ezekiel, he says they looked like four animals with four heads and wings, and there were fiery wheels among them. He says, they were under a vault that gleamed like crystal, and there was a throne-shaped sapphire hanging over the vault. And in the sapphire was a man who burned from the loins downward." Crick closed his Bible and sat back, his flowing grey beard jutting toward Paterson. "Now, when Doctor Jon Paterson gets on the podium at the university to describe the same thing, what does *he* say?"

Paterson's interest was obvious, but so was his noncomprehension. "I don't know what you're getting at, Captain."

"Doctor Paterson, son, says: 'I saw a landing craft descend and disgorge four passengers, while the pilot stayed aboard. The passengers appeared to be extraterrestrials, insectoid and exoskeletal. They wore atmosphere-inhibiting helmets and appeared to be surrounded by a force field of an electrical nature. The pilot spoke to us through an amplifier.' "

Paterson was sitting bolt upright, his mouth open in an "O." Rebecca Martin jumped in front of her grandfather. "Josiah," she cried, genuinely shocked. "That's blasphemous!"

"Is it, child?"

"It *is*. How can you even suggest that God's angels—"

"I'm not." Crick was enjoying himself. "I'm simply stating a parallel between Doctor Paterson's, ah, creatures, and Ezekiel's visions."

"But Poppa-Bear, you're sounding like all those stupid apologists of the last century, the ones who kept trying to explain the Bible by scientific rationale. You don't really believe any of that, do you?"

"I believe that the Lord in His wisdom doesn't give us a burden we can't bear, Becky. Now, just suppose what Ezekiel saw *was* an ex-tee race, come to visit Earth. Old Ezekiel, he wouldn't have the frame of reference to handle that idea, would he? He'd have to interpret what he saw in the terms he could understand, and which his people could understand." He looked to Paterson for confirmation.

Paterson's face registered a wary interest. "That's a pretty liberal view for a fundamentalist. I thought you Baptists took the Bible word-for-word literally?"

"We Baptists take the Word of God literally, son, and the Word's been through a powerful number of interpretations since it was first given to us. But the Message keeps getting through, no matter what the language or the translation."

Rebecca jumped into the conversation again, almost bouncing in her agitation. "Yes, but you're still implying that what Ezekiel saw was mortal instead of the messengers of God."

"Am I?" Crick asked mildly. "Remember that comparisons work both ways, child."

It took a minute, but both Paterson and the woman saw it. Paterson chuckled nervously. "Are you trying to convince me, Crick, that the Lorsii are angels, and that I'm being sent these previews of their invasion by God?"

Crick stroked his beard. "Well, they don't sound much like angels, do they? But remember that God has all creation at His command. And if He can send angels to carry His message to Ezekiel—seein's how angels were something Ezekiel could understand and accept—why can't He send an alien race to carry His message to you—seein's how you can't accept angels?"

The old sailor turned to his controls and put the 'liner in motion, satisfied that he had planted a seed of thought in Jon Paterson's mind. A seed which, if tended carefully, might grow into something powerful in the service of God.

* * * *

Outside Blama Town, an ox-drawn altar wagon accepted converts into the Army of the Final Testament. The oxen, freed of towing the wagon, plodded on a circular boom, generating electricity for the lines which led into the wagon itself. Two Army noncoms, their facial scars identifying them as Mandingos from farther north, welcomed the initiates with friendly smiles and miss-nothing eyes.

Among the would-be Zlotnyites was a boy on crutches. He hobbled up the ramp and into the wagon, kneeling before the altar as he was told to do and looking awed by the stormy-sky hologram projected behind it. A naked girl, her left breast tattooed with Zlotney's horned cross, laid her hands on the boy's temples. Her palms were cool against his forehead; cool and dry and electrified. Beneath her skin, wires and electrodes had been implanted. They ran up her arms and into a tiny box implanted in her breast. Other wires led out of the box, down her side, and to her right foot, where two copper contacts were exposed. The box in her breast, should she be captured or questioned, would explode and reduce everything in a twelve-meter radius to ash. The contacts on her foot connected her to a sensitive set of instruments in the back of the wagon. These instruments measured the emotional and glandular output of the person whose forehead the girl caressed. As she touched the boy with the crutches, red lights lit on the instruments in the back.

She caused the boy to stand and led him around the altar. The Army's hymn filled the air. Red velvet curtains parted, showing what appeared to be a garden of carnal delights, with a sculpted couch in the foreground. Voluptuous persons of indeterminate sex bade the boy enter.

He stepped forward and died.

But the one-shot shortwave transmitter in his crutches got off a quick burst of information first. The snap of coded information, traveling at the speed of light, reached out in a globe a kilometer in diameter before it ceased. Within that globe, it was picked up by a fisherman out in the river, and he died by lasershot. It was picked up by a fat old woman with a market basket on her head, and she died with her back against a tree, shouting the Gospel as she struck at the Army soldiers who finally beat her to the ground. It was picked up by a man who had lain buried in a box under the lionbrush for six days, waiting, and he died as soldiers poured gasoline on his box and lit it.

And it was picked up by a small, atomic capsule strapped to the leg of an African swallow which flew amid a flock of companions nearby. And it lived, undetected, and flew on, its flight directed by electrodes and implants. It flew to exhaustion and fell to the earth, where a Masai herdsman picked it and the capsule up and carried them south. Along the way, the herdsman shed his loincloth and spear, replaced them with a business jumper and a pair of glasses, and caught one of the few commercial planes still flying, which took him to the burnt-out but still controlled city of Johannesburg.

In a WorldGov office building there, people with serious faces decoded the capsule, translated the information into several languages, and recoded it again. It was sent to every WorldGov command center still functioning, and these centers in turn sent it out to every person, group, or organization which could still be counted on to be in the fight against Ibrihim Zlotny. The information made no sense in and of itself; just a collection of impressions and images, and a few statistics on the altar wagon and its contents. But perhaps it would fill some niche in the puzzle or spark some insight.

The information went by armed courier from the radio room of the Alberta Experimental Facility to the office of the director, where Lee Hardin signed for it and began studying it. For some time his perusal was perfunctory. Despite the calamity of Zlotny, he was still a doctor and had a hospital full of sick people to run. He had little belief that his contribution—if any—would prove vital in the fight against the moon-faced evangelist.

Then he felt himself go cold. Sweat stood out on his face and he fumbled for the intercom. "Would you get Doctor Marvis in here, please, right away?"

She came a minute or so later, still wearing a stethoscope and carrying her rounds bag. "Something up, Lee?"

"Annie, look what just came in from WorldGov."

She bent over the desk, her arm lightly around his shoulders. "What is it?"

"A readout that some agent got from inside one of Zlotny's altar trucks. See, it proves definitely that he uses electronics in his conversions."

"Well, we were pretty sure of that already."

"Right. Now, look at this. It's an enhancement—just like we use here. It seems to be some kind of subliminal visual projection they do, screened out by those holos of storms and do-it-yourself brothels. Look at the images."

Doctor Marvis looked. "Okay, phobic images interspersed with benevolent ones. Looks as if he's trying to blur the mental line between good and evil. Common enough technique. The Chinese used it during their brainwash experiments."

"Yeah, but look close at this one, the one that keeps repeating. What do you see?"

"A guy in a cape? A frogman? I don't know."

"What you're looking at, Annie, is one of Jon Paterson's Lorsii." Hardin's voice was filled with dread.

Doctor Marvis sat down. "Oh, dear. That's not possible. How could those people have any connection with Jon's dreams?"

"They don't," Hardin said grimly. "He's somehow been getting leakage from them. Somehow or other, Jon's been receiving their broadcasts."

"Then he's not insane."

"No. It's worse than that. He's right."

"What do you mean, 'right'?"

Hardin came around the desk. "Don't you see it, Annie? It all makes sense now: Zlotny and his zombies and Jon's Lorsii and everything. The Lorsii are real! They're behind Zlotny. They're how he gets his power and does his tricks. They must be signaling him some way, and Jon's managed to get on the circuit somehow."

Marvis fumbled in her bag. "Lee," she said carefully, "what if you're right?"

"Then we're being set up for an invasion, just as Jon said. We've got to let the authorities know."

"They won't believe you, any more than you believed Jon."

"I'll make them."

"No, I don't think you will, Lee." Marvis' hand came out of the bag with a hypodermic in it. Before Hardin could move, she had grabbed his arm, turned the forearm up, and inserted the needle in a vein. "It's just air, Lee. A simple embolism. You won't feel anything at all."

Hardin jerked back, but it was too late. "Annie, for God's sake—" Then the air bubbles reached his heart, and he fell, dead before he hit the floor.

Marvis stood and closed her bag. "Not God's sake, Lee. For the Left Hand and the salvation of the world." She placed her bag neatly on the floor and hit the intercom. "Please send a cardiac unit to Dr. Hardin's office. He seems to have had a seizure." Of course, the unit would be too late for Lee Hardin, just as his warning would have been too late for Earth.

* * * *

Zlotny's armada came up from Oklahoma with leisurely disdain for the sporadic bombardments of rockets, lasers, and suicide pilots which tried to penetrate its outer rings and reach the single, all-important copter in the center. Nothing got closer than several kilometers. At one point, the vast sphere of weaponry and fanatics passed directly over the Milk & Honey, whose occupants did not even see Zlotny's copter, any more than the self-styled evangelist saw them. The 'liner registered on many instruments in the armada, though. On radar screens and infrared detectors and mass-analyzers. Hard eyes watched the instruments, and computers tracked the 'liner with the ugly snouts of gun batteries. Procedures were put in motion, messages flew between the aircraft and the ground, and by the time Zlotny's machine had deposited him at the NASA installation in Manitou Springs, a brief on the 'liner and its occupants was already written and on its way to the command room.

Zlotny made his way through the faithful and into his personal quarters, where he refreshed himself and was bathed by novices. When he appeared in the command room, he was buoyant, relaxed, and obviously pleased with himself and the way his crusade was going. He listened to the briefing officer, a crew-cut, elderly man with the intensity of the true believer, while sipping tea and toying with a small, hook-studded whip. The briefing went on for some time before something caught Zlotny's ear. "Read that again, servant," he ordered.

The man paused, studied the briefs again, and cleared his throat. "A freightliner is reported in the mountains north of Raton Pass. Recon photos make her the Milk & Honey, an old machine registered to one E.J. Crick. The vessel is apparently making its way in our direction."

Zlotny scratched the studded whip back and forth across the

top of the desk beside his chair. "And why was this included in your report, servant? Surely the Left Hand's forces can deal with a freightliner. That doesn't sound like the most formidable sortie our enemies are making against us."

"This Crick, sir, is a known preacher, a sworn enemy of the Duality. Further, he has with him a man named Jon Paterson who, it is reported, is insane and is obsessed with destroying you." He paused and looked up. "We did not want to trouble you with this, sir, but a servant in Canada—now martyred—reported that this Paterson seems to have some sort of vague comprehension of...our friends."

Zlotny's whip stopped abruptly. His eyebrows went up his forehead, and he had a slightly bemused expression on his face. "So...! Perhaps it is well that you have taken notice of this pair." He held out a pudgy hand. "Let me have that brief, servant. You've done a good job."

Zlotny dismissed the man and sat for a time studying the brief closely. Then he rose and went into a darkened, sulphurous, chamber where he sat crosslegged on a cushion and placed a horned metal band around his head. He flipped switches on a small box beside the cushion. "Beloved master," he whispered. "Thy servant seeks thy counsel."

* * * *

CHAPTER NINE

Paterson eased the *Milk & Honey* into the shadows beneath a stand of pine and brought her to a stop. "Let's take a break. We're going to have to be sharp from here on."

They were in the mountains above Raton Pass, less than a hundred kilometers from Zlotny's personal domain at Manitou. They had been dodging patrols for the past six hours, and henceforth the risk of discovery would increase exponentially for every meter they covered. Rebecca could not believe they had not been detected already and was skeptical of both her grandfather's explanation that the Lord's hand was blinding their enemies and Paterson's that the zombies were too confident to bother looking. She clambered down the ladder after the two men, feeling as though a million hostile eyes were watching her. "I don't think it's a good idea to be out in the open like this."

Neither man paid any attention. Both were deep inside themselves, like gladiators before a battle. But it was obvious their adversary was outside, for they both unconsciously faced Pikes Peak, barely visible in the distance, on whose slopes the Army of the Final Testament had its dark fortress. Rebecca placed herself between the men, her hands on her hips. "I *said*, I don't think it's too bright to be out here in the open like this."

Paterson blinked, stretching hugely. "It's cramped in there, Rebecca. We're all tired. We need to walk around awhile, get some fresh air into our lungs. May be the last chance we get for a while."

"Yeah, like forever. Are you planning on knocking first or just barging in? Couldn't be more than half a million of them up there. Shouldn't be much of a problem for the Lone Ranger and Tonto, huh?"

Crick raised a calming hand. "Now, Becky, child."

"Oh, hell, Grandpa!"

"Please, don't swea—"

"Poppa-Bear, this is the last chance. Any second now a mob of howling fanatics is going to jump out of the trees and dismember us."

"I think perhaps they would take us into custody."

"Like they did the people in Prescott, or Amarillo, or that village back there where all the little girls had been—"

Paterson shushed her. "Easy, easy. We're all tight. Let's take a walk, calm down, think. Maybe we won't have to go in after all."

Rebecca's surprise made her mouth drop. "That is the only sensible thing you've said since I've known you." As if to keep him from changing his mind, she took her grandfather's arm. "C'mon, let's walk."

He nodded, but gently removed his elbow. "Let us find our separate solitudes, child. I think I would like to pray awhile." So saying, he walked off into the trees.

"Not, far, Grandpa! Stay close!" She watched anxiously a moment, then turned to Paterson. "Do you think he'll get lost?"

"A sailor, lost?"

She looked from Paterson to the trees, biting her lip, then walked off at a slight angle to the path her grandfather had taken, trying to respect his need for privacy while still keeping near him.

Once in the trees, she felt a strange premonition and found herself turning back. She paused behind a fallen log, feeling a little silly at spying on Paterson, but doing so anyway. He was sitting against a tire, apparently writing something in a small notebook. Presently he rose and went up the ladder. A moment later he came down again carrying Hezekiah under one arm. He sat the animal on the ground and tucked a piece of paper under its collar. Then he went lightly back up the ladder. A moment later the *Milk & Honey* began to roll down the slope toward Raton Pass, coasting silently with the servos off.

Rebecca Martin felt conflicting emotions wash over her. She wanted to yell for him to stop, wanted to yell for him to come back, wanted to yell in thanksgiving that he was going and her grandfather wasn't, wanted to curse him for stealing her home. And in the end, she stuffed her fist in her mouth, made a kind of waving gesture, and found herself uttering a silent prayer for the safety of the strange, hateful, brave man piloting the 'liner down the mountain.

She ran into the clearing and scooped up Hezekiah. Beelzebub blinked fearfully from the cat's thick fur. She took out the folded note and read it, nodding occasionally. "Okay, Doctor," she said softly. "We'll play it that way." Cuddling Hezekiah to her breast, she set out at a near trot toward her grandfather.

But Elmer Josiah Crick was nowhere to be found.

* * * *

In a darkness reeking of sulphur, Ibrihim Zlotny sat crosslegged, his hooded, oriental eyes slitted and a small, tight smile on his face. There was a humming sound in the blackness, as of a muted dynamo. Every now and again there would be a sharp, crackling snap, and actinic stutters of sparks leapt from unseen sources to the tips of golden horns banded to his head. At each snapping strike, Zlotny appeared to gather a power into himself. Finally, he arched his back, his smile widening into a feral grin. "Yes," he murmured. "Yes, there you are. Now I come for you."

In the forest a hundred kilometers away, Captain Crick staggered upright from where he knelt in prayer, clutching his head in his hands, his face contorted. He marched as if he were a puppet toward a jutting outcrop of rock whose near side was sloped and mossy and whose far edge was a precipice. He made inarticulate grunts, half anger, half pain. His stiff legs carried him up the mossed slope toward the sheer drop. He grabbed his thighs as if to halt them, then grabbed at a bush only to find his fingers, somehow, would not close around the branch.

At the very edge of the drop he stopped, swaying drunkenly. His face was rivered with sweat, and he trembled in eccentric, cyclic spasms. But his eyes showed no fear, only an intense aliveness, almost an exultation.

A voice sounded, perhaps in the air, perhaps in Crick's skull.

"So, old sailor, you would come for me, would you? All the way from the terrible cold north."

Crick's fists clinched and opened, clinched and opened. But his voice was calm. "I go where the Lord directs me."

"And He has directed you to come in such hate and rage to me, a mere servant of him in whom you do not even believe?"

"The Lord has sent me to deal with Satan in all his limbs and members, Zlotny."

"Such a frail warrior!"

"Not much of an enemy, perhaps. God seems to think I'm 'bout all that's needed for the likes of you."

After a moment, the voice laughed nastily. "Perhaps you're a little stronger than you appear, old man. That's good! The Left Hand enjoys a worthy adversary."

Crick took a cautious step back from the edge of the drop-off. Instantly, he was forced stiff-legged back to the brink. Zlotny's mocking voice appeared hurt. "Now, Captain; to come all this way only to rush off? I have been looking forward to chatting with you, you know."

Crick licked his lips. "How do you know me? How did you know we were coming?"

"We? You would make a poor gambler. Did I know there were others in your party? Did I know Jon Paterson was coming in his rage and madness? Did I know your emotional but loving granddaughter was with you? You give too much away, old man. How did you ever succeed as a trader?"

"A few simple tricks you wouldn't know about, Zlotny. Honest deals. Respect for my customers. Fair work for fair money."

"Ah, yes. The Christian ideal." There was an ugly glee in the voice. "That's the same ideal which created the manifest destiny that allowed the Europeans to steal this land from the Indians, isn't it? I recall reading how the Congress prayed for the 'enlightenment' of the 'savages' while signing the orders which would destroy them as a people. That ideal, umm?"

"No. The Christian ideal was what drove preachers and editors and citizens to resist the government in print and public, even though they knew it would do no good. *That* ideal sent missionaries onto the reservations with books and food and medicine, even when the Indians thought they were no different than the rest of the white men an' massacred them by the dozens. Even when the government harassed them and had them shot and tried to disband their churches." Crick's voice was growing stronger. "Most anybody can call himself a Christian, Zlotny, and a powerful lot of evil has been done in the name of Christ. But not by real Christians." Crick threw his chin defiantly heavenward, as if searching the treetops for Zlotny. "If th' best you can do for arguments is the old chestnut 'bout murdering for God, maybe th' Lord could have sent somebody else after you—like maybe a child."

There was a moment of terrible pressure on Crick. He was washed in a wave of pure hatred and found himself being propelled the last step to the cliff. Then the pressure stopped. Zlotny's voice was cunning, smooth. "Ah, yes, a child. Now, that could be interesting. Suppose the child was your granddaughter, old man? Suppose the Duality in its wisdom decided she could best be of service as my concubine? She *is* a pretty little scut. It would be interesting, I think, to have her naked beneath me. Perhaps tied to my bed, umm? I could arrange for you to watch, Captain? Or even participate! Surely your juices haven't dried up so much that you couldn't appreciate that? All those long nights in your freighter, just you and her? There must have been many times you caught a glimpse of her as she prepared for bed." Zlotny's voice went off into a chuckle.

Crick's own smile was small and somehow sad. "One of th' differences between Christians and people like you, Zlotny, is that we don't *have* t' tie our mates up. See, once you know the joy of honest love, you're forever freed of th' need for the kind of warped, ugly lusts a worm like you needs."

Crick snorted. "You want Rebecca? I suppose you can take her. But she's a Christian. You'd get no satisfaction out of her—nor me. Christians have a lot of experience at watching their loved ones be soiled by evil."

"If I recall, the Nazis were Christian."

"No, just hidin' behind th' title. An' nobody ever claimed Christians had any corner on the suffering market. There were Christian Germans hidin' Jews during that war, an' there's Jews hidin' Christians durin' this one. It's always been that way, Zlotny, an' always will be. Th' good folks hang together when something like you crawls out from under a rock. That's what's always whipped your kind, an' what always will."

There was silence for a time. Crick stood on the edge of the cliff with the wind whipping his beard. His hands were at his side, and it wasn't clear if he was still held on that vast drop or just standing there.

Then the moment passed and Zlotny's evil wrapped around him again. The insidious voice came once again. "Do you believe in your faith, Crick?"

"Of course."

"Do you believe that your God will save you if I march you off this rock?"

"If that's His will, yes."

"Can you think of a single incidence of His doing so in all history? Can you name me one person who's ever stepped into the air and been saved by the Hand of God?"

"No."

"And you still believe?"

"Yes."

"Then, old man, I shall walk you off this rock."

Crick's smile was even smaller and sadder. He shook his head.

"No, you won't."

"And why not, pray tell—if you'll pardon my pun?"

"Because," Crick said very softly, "you can't."

The silence was longer this time, and deadly. "*Can't?* Can't! I brought you here. Even now I am bringing Jon Paterson to my fortress. And if I desire her, I will bring your granddaughter to my bed."

"You can't do it, Zlotny," Crick said, as though explaining something to a person of small intelligence, "because the Lord God has ordered me to be your destruction. And that time's not come yet."

"Walk, Crick! Walk!"

"No."

For several seconds, the air about Josiah Crick was blue with sparks and lightning. Nearby bushes caught fire. The rock sizzled. In his head, Crick felt a horrible weight of obscene, cursed hatred.

Then he was alone in the heat and smoke.

"Grandpa! Poppa-Bear!"

He turned in time to catch Rebecca in his arms before she stumbled off the cliff. "Well, child. Calm down, now. What's all the fuss?"

"Fuss! You run off and get lost in these woods, and I find you in the middle of a forest fire, and Paterson's stolen the *Milk & Honey*, and I was worried out of my mind for you, and—"

"Slow down, now. Back engines, girl." He put an arm around her shoulder and guided her off the rock. "It's all right. It's all right."

"Yes, it is. That fool Paterson—"

"Don't curse the man, Becky."

"He's stolen our ship and gone after Zlotny."

"I know."

"He left us this—how did you know that? You two didn't plan it, did you?"

"No. Someone else did." He took the paper from her, scratched Hezekiah, and shoved his glasses out to the end of his nose. "Hmm. 'Sorry to do this to you, but I have to get to Zlotny's communications facilities. The Lorsii are coming. There's a town called Dos Rios two hundred klicks east, with a big lake north of it. Halfway around the lake is a limestone cave. You can't find it unless you have this map I've drawn. I used to fish there, and have the cave stocked with provisions. You should last a long time. I'm sorry. Thanks for all you've done.'" Crick folded the note and pocketed it. "Well, well. Jon has the right instincts, anyway."

Rebecca looked hopeful. "Then we're going? You're not going to Manitou Springs?"

"For th' moment, child, I think we'd do best to follow Jon's advice." He offered her his arm, as though he were escorting her on a stroll through a park. "Sometimes the Lord's ways are mysterious, but His instructions never are. They're always clear as a calm river to those who are prepared to listen to them." He made a show of helping her over a small boulder, neither of them seeming to notice that it was her arm which took the weight and not his. "Now, our friend Jon, for example. He's received a set of instructions from God. Only he can't see it that way, so he thinks he's got to warn the world about this invasion."

Becky blew out a breath. "Whew! For a while I was afraid you'd begun to believe all that guff about bugs from outer space."

"Oh, I do, Becky. I do. Matter of fact, I been expecting the invasion for two or three days now."

She stopped, confused. "Grandpa?"

"Y'see, Paterson thinks Zlotny's a pawn of the Lorsii. You think Zlotny's as crazy as you think me and Jon are."

"I never said that, Poppa-Bear."

"But the truth is, child, that all of us—you, me, Paterson, Zlotny, and the Lorsii—are moving at the will of God and by His grace. The Lord has called up Armageddon with Zlotny as His tool and the Lorsii as His weapons, for even as they are directed by Satan, Satan is part of God's creation and thus is His servant." He stopped for a moment beside a tiny stream running down through the pines. "I don't know Paterson's part in God's plan for the battle, but I suspect it won't end with this attack on Zlotny's fortress." He looked his granddaughter in the eyes, his face calm and elated. "But the Lord has seen fit to show me my part—which is to destroy the great enemy's servant, Zlotny—and I know that nothing Jon Paterson does will affect that. Now or later, here or somewhere else, I shall face Ibrihim Zlotny and somehow conquer him." He smiled gently. "Now, let's walk. It's a long way to Dos Rios. I was there once, back in '26, when I was a helmsman on the *Pride of Weehawken*. In those days, th' town was mostly fishin'." He rambled on as they made their way back down the mountains toward the high plains of Texas.

* * * *

The six officers of the Army of the Final Testament wore expressions ranging from disbelief to annoyance. They were gathered around a table in Zlotny's quarters, in a tight little room still smelling faintly of sulphur, and had just heard their leader tell them to void their plans for the destruction of the *Milk & Honey* and its crew.

"But why, Great Servant?" one asked, unable to mask his frustration.

Zlotny's smile was both benevolent and cunning. "Is it not sufficient that I order it so, servant?"

The officer licked his lips and dropped his eyes. "Of course," he said softly. "Yours is the Voice of the Duality."

"Even so." Zlotny laughed, an oddly merry sound in that evil place. "But it is not my desire to thwart your efforts, General Carrick. Nor to deprive you of your, ah, entertainment."

The officer's face rearranged itself into appreciation and a kind of anticipation which boded ill for the *Milk & Honey.* "Great Servant, I perceive your wisdom exceeds my own shortsightedness. You have, then, a plan?"

"I always have a plan, little servant." Zlotny settled back in his chair as his generals inched forward, their faces alight. "I have spoken with the Left Hand," Zlotny said, noting with satisfaction the automatic ritual gestures the officers made and the slight tinge of awe and fear which flitted through their eyes. Timing the moment, playing the men as though they were an instrument, Zlotny spaced his revelations. "This man Paterson. He is of use to the Hand. We are going to allow him to come among us."

There came a rash of oaths and exclamations. "Sir! Your safety!"

"I trust in your efficiency, gentlemen, to protect my worthless person. Your efficiency and my own planning." He leaned forward, pinning each of them with his eyes. "We shall allow this Paterson person to come to us—to me. We shall allow him to bring his hatred and revenge and killing drive into the presence of the Great Servant. But—" His smile was openly malicious, now. "But. We shall insure that this Paterson who reaches us is not quite the same one who is even now coming."

An officer raised a hand. "But, Sir, as I understand it, Paterson is not actually after you. He wants to use the broadcast station to tell the world about our, er, allies."

"Quite true, quite true. And why, Colonel Monaghan?" Without awaiting an answer, he went on. "Because friend Paterson fears and despises our allies, yes? But suppose his feelings are, mmm, reoriented? Suppose he is not quite so sure of those feelings by the time he gets here?"

They looked puzzled. "How can we change his feelings?"

"You ask that, after our accomplishments with the cattle of the earth?"

General Carrick cleared his throat. "Could I presume to ask why the Great Servant desires that this should all come to pass? Would it not be simpler—and safer for you—to just dispose of him now?"

"Simpler, yes. But less useful. It is not I who desire him here, General. It is the express wish of the Left Hand."

In the silence which followed this revelation, Zlotny prepared to drop his final bomb. "Gentlemen, let us prepare a path for friend Paterson. Let us not make it too easy, but not impossible, either. Let us assure that Paterson has...suitable adventures on his way to our little fortress. You will arrange this, using expendable soldiers." He rose, resting the fingers of both hands lightly on the table. "I, meanwhile, shall return to my communion with the allies, and shall thus insure the needed change in Paterson's frame of reference. We shall time his arrival here to coincide with another arrival. One which we have all awaited and longed for many, many months."

The men in the room stiffened in fear and surprise. "Y-you mean—"

"Even so, servant, even so." And with that, Zlotny left them.

* * * *

Jon Paterson lay on the roof of the *Milk & Honey*, flattened against the metal plates with his head as low as possible. Below him a squad of soldiers of the Army of the Final Testament was working its way cautiously up the hill, keeping behind the cover of the bushes and rocks. Paterson made them seven, but could not be sure there weren't more. In his hand he clutched the 'liner's flare pistol. If he could just get one of their rifles....

The squad fanned out and advanced on the clearing where the 'liner sat as though abandoned. After a time, a soldier fired a round through the pilot's window of the cabin, almost experimentally. Paterson lay still and hardly breathing atop the machine.

A soldier rose, cautiously, and advanced into the clearing. Paterson eased the flare pistol over the forward edge of the roof, both hands locked on the grip. The pistol had no sights, but at this range a hit was certain. He began to squeeze gently on the trigger.

There was a sharp, dizzying pain just behind his eyes. "Ah, how sweet to kill!"

Paterson felt himself grow cold. He knew that voice. Knew it from newstapes, from the radio. And he knew, without quite knowing how, that it was in his head, was put there, that he was not hallucinating. He formulated a wave of silent hatred. "Get out of my skull, you bastard!"

"Just an ounce more pressure, Jon Paterson. An ounce more on the trigger and that ball of burning phosphorous will fly out and strike that soldier in the chest. Think how sweet! The soldier's coming to kill you, Jon Paterson. Coming to make a flaming ruin of your own life and body. You must kill him in self-defense."

"Out, you slug. Leave me alone." Paterson continued to increase the pressure on the trigger.

"Of course, if you weren't coming to me, if you were minding your own business, if you were defending your home, it wouldn't be murder."

Paterson's finger eased.

"Yes. Murder. After all, the soldier's only doing his job. You are the enemy here, Jon Paterson, aren't you?"

Paterson pressed his sweating forehead into the cool metal of the 'liner roof, gritting his teeth. "Get out of me, you animal," he thought viciously. "It won't work, damn you!" He raised his head again, sighting down the pistol barrel.

"Look, Jon. The soldier's a girl. What is she, fifteen, perhaps? A schoolgirl. Maybe you could just wound her. A leg wound. Picture yourself undressing her, bathing her wound. Who knows what form her gratitude would take, uh? But then, wounded as she would be, you wouldn't have to worry about gratitude. You could take what you wanted."

Paterson felt confused, filled with impotent rage and with fright. He shook himself.

The girl saw the motion. Her rifle cracked and splashed sharp metal across Paterson's cheek.

Without thought, Paterson fired. The flare caught her in the stomach. She fell backward without a sound, her body flaming.

With an inarticulate howl, Paterson flung himself down through the hatch into the cabin. Bullets and laser beams spattered the body of the tractor, splintering the glass of the windscreens. He threw the switches and jammed the accelerator. The *Milk & Honey* lurched forward down the hill while Paterson tried with all his soul not to see the burning girl over whose body he was passing.

In his head, Paterson heard Zlotny's mocking laughter. "Thou shalt not kill, Doctor. It's against the oath. Thou shalt *not!* It's against the Biblical law. But didn't it feel good, Jon Paterson? Didn't it, just for an instant, feel *good*?" * * * *

"Stand by, stand by." The corporal's eyes were hard and elated. He surveyed the squad gathered around him. The oldest among them was seventeen. "Have you made your peace?"

A savage yell of affirmation.

"You are ready for transformation?"

Another.

The corporal nodded in grim satisfaction. "You know your jobs?"

A girl stepped forward. "I will entice him."

"And if he accepts, if he stops?"

"I will die."

Again, the grim nod. The corporal turned to the next soldier. "You?"

The boy snapped to attention. "I will offer friendship. I will come out unarmed and stand before him."

"And?"

"I will throw myself beneath the wheels of his machine."

"If he stops?"

"I will attack him and force him to kill me."

One by one, the squad detailed their assignments, each speaking in tones of exaltation of his or her coming death, each seeing beyond the moment of dissolution to the forever of evil delights offered by Zlotny's Left Hand, each suffused with visions of endless revenges against a life which had somehow wronged him, of acts for which he had been punished, thoughts of which he had felt ashamed, urges unfulfilled for fear of reprisals. One saw an eon of torturing small animals, another an age of rolling in things unclean, a third of endlessly smashing her mother's head in.

For Zlotny taught a warped version of eye-for-an-eye justice. He taught that vengeance was yours forever, if only you were willing to be the victim once—in the cause of the Left Hand. By your death, your pain and humiliation for a brief, searing instant, you bought yourself the right to inflict upon others your vilest desires for all the long length of eternity. And each among the squad of fanatics believed this with desperate militancy. And not a face among them betrayed any consciousness of immorality as they set forth—as hundreds of others were doing—to throw their lives away before Jon Paterson's eyes, so that he might come to Ibrihim Zlotny a confused and unbalanced man.

* * * *

Jon Paterson brought the *Milk & Honey* down out of Raton Pass and through the ravines, northwest to Colorado Springs. The land around him was despoiled, the outlying farms and businesses gutted. Everywhere, carrion birds blackened the sky as they flapped from one grisly feast to another. A pall of smoke lay over the ground, undulating in and out among the hills like a greasy shroud. Here and there a once-human figure hung from some makeshift gibbet or sagged from spikes driven through wrists and ankles. The stench was overwhelming.

But Paterson barely saw any of this, barely saw the freeway his huge 'liner was straddling. His vision was a haloed tunnel and there was fire in his brain. Behind him lay the nightmare encounters Ibrihim Zlotny had set up, a stop-frame series of images of dead and dying bodies, of gunshots and flame and lasers. And the endless, nagging, vile voice in his head.

He knew he was being led to Zlotny, knew the fights had been shams, knew he was being toyed with. But it didn't matter. He'd get to the fat little man. He'd get there and crush the life out of him before he faced the cameras and warned the earth.

Soldiers of the Army of the Final Testament moved across his path from time to time, but none tried to stop him. The charade was over. Paterson drove unmolested into Colorado Springs. He parked the *Milk & Honey* beside the freeway and climbed down. A station wagon with bullet holes in its doors and Zlotny's emblem crudely painted on the sides pulled up. A boy stepped out. "Please come with us. The Great Servant is waiting."

Docile, Paterson climbed into the vehicle's back seat and sat numbly as the car drove to Manitou Springs. Zlotny's troops were everywhere, manning gun emplacements, standing idly in groups, marching from place to place. The car passed a group of five soldiers who didn't look up from raping a woman.

But this was all background noise for Paterson. His mind was a screaming, incandescent light. And in the light was a voice and a glory, a power and a presence. Be calm; all goes according to plan; all is known. And weaving through the light, the passing input, the hiss of pain and fear and hatred and excitement, was a black, bitter-cold thread of future memories: boats sailing a frozen sea; the old man running, running; a bright, hideous arrow....

They came to a building, and Paterson was taken out of the station wagon. His guards pointed to the door, then walked off. Paterson was alone and ignored in the heart of the enemy citadel. On the steps of the building, a girl lay in drunken sleep, her uniform soiled and torn. Paterson scooped up her rifle and walked into the darkness.

* * * *

In London, the West End burned unattended. Frightened people scurried from building to building, watching for Zlotny's soldiers. Every now and again, some man working his family furtively out of the city would spot a patrol and tense, raising his pistol or hoe handle or bed stave and shielding his loved ones. Then he would lower the weapon in perplexity as the patrol passed by, its members oblivious to all around them, their faces filled with rapture and their eyes on the heavens.

In Karachi a twice-raped boy cowered against his dead father and closed his eyes. He did not see that the burly lieutenant was paying him no attention, nor that the soldier was chanting in a deep, slurred voice, unmindful of where he walked.

In Kobe, the bartender crept from behind his wine barrels in wonder as every last Zlotnyite laid down the tools with which they had been wrecking his place and filed out into the street, moving as if they were blind.

All over the world, Zlotny's billions left off their destruction and pillage. They moved entranced into the streets and onto the highways, and all began converging on a few hundred sites.

* * * *

"Ah, Doctor Paterson, please come in. I've been expecting you." Ibrihim Zlotny stood before a large mirror, being helped into a set of scarlet robes by two naked boys. "I have to congratulate you on finding your way to my quarters. That was really the hard part, you know; this building is very badly laid out."

Paterson stood in the doorway, a laser rifle in his hands. As Zlotny turned to face him, he raised the weapon and centered its sights on Zlotny's round face. Zlotny smiled back at him with genuine pleasure. "Lasers are so much less messy than projectile weapons, don't you think? Cauterize as they destroy the flesh." He walked toward Paterson. "Come, I'll take you to the broadcast room."

Paterson felt the weapon waver in his hands. As Zlotny walked to and then past him, he lowered the piece, then tossed it to the floor. He followed Zlotny into the hall.

"We really had a time keeping up with you, Doctor," Zlotny said conversationally, slowing to allow Paterson to catch up. "Even with our facilities we lost you for a time, up in South Dakota. Nature is so much better at hiding things than we are at finding them, um?"

The analytic part of Paterson's mind was forcing itself into prominence. The ringing and the light were still there, but they no longer dominated. Paterson found himself noticing things: Zlotny's shortness, the smell of the hallway, the sound of their footsteps. "Why did you bring me here?" he asked, surprised that the question had come, fully formed, from his lips.

"It was your desire to warn the people of the earth about an impending disaster, I believe. I enjoy helping people achieve their goals."

"The Lorsii are real, aren't they?" Paterson's demand was fierce.

Zlotny came to a room and stood aside, courteously motioning Paterson in ahead of him. "What is reality, Doctor? At one time, all reality was the physical world of the Mediterranean, and no one knew what lay beyond the pillars of Hercules."

Paterson blocked the door. "They're real, and they're coming."

Zlotny grinned and stepped around Paterson. "Come, let us make use of the facilities which have brought you so very far."

The broadcast room was filled with Zlotnyites, all with the strange exultation on their faces. They knelt as the two men entered, and Paterson had the odd feeling that they were paying homage to him as much as to Zlotny.

"As this is my facility, Doctor, I shall claim first rights before the camera. You may speak after I have finished."

Paterson started forward but was stopped by two boys who looked perfectly capable of restraining him. He subsided.

Zlotny chatted as a girl placed gold-plated horns on his balding forehead. He seemed aware that Paterson wasn't listening to him, but it did not appear to matter. At a flick of his finger, the girl retreated and every face in the room turned to him. He beamed. "Are you prepared, my friends? Are your souls ready to receive the Left Hand?"

A shout of yeses barked through the room.

"Are you ready for the might and majesty? The terrible presence?"

Another shout.

"Even if you be among the chosen, among the sacrifices?"

The answering shout seemed almost eager.

Zlotny stepped in front of the camera, his arms spread wide and his own face suffused now with exultation. The light on the camera winked on, and all over the earth a billion loudspeakers, a billion screens carried Zlotny's image and voice. And the voice was not the bland, amused voice the people of earth had come to know and either love or fear for the past months, but the voice of power and terror. It rang and clanged with resonances of things unspeakable, of triumphs over the helpless and gloating over the suffering of others. It hissed and crawled and cackled. "Sinners!" Zlotny cried, "Thy hour is at hand! Now comes the Left Hand. Ye who would not believe; ye who remained blind in your fear and ignorance; ye who worshiped but half the Duality; ye who resisted; ye who shut your faces to the bliss of the darkness! Now shall you reap what you have sown."

Zlotny seemed to grow. His eyes flashed magnetic fire. Spittle flew from his lips. It seemed to Paterson that a smell of sulphur filled the room.

"And ye faithful; ye bearers of the crimson brand; ye who have walked the lefthand path with me; ye destroyers of the false and faithless; ye despoilers of the sanctimonious, the self-righteous, the pious; ye soldiers of the Army of the Final Testament: now come you into your kingdom. For behold, even as you hear my words, the servants of the Left Hand come among men. Look ye, sinners and faithful; look to the sky!"

The monitor screen in the broadcast room blanked out, and Ibrihim Zlotny's image was replaced by a view of a cloud-studded blue sky. And in that sky were jewels: rubies and emeralds and diamonds, all of a light and a glitter to burn the eye. And the jewels fell toward the earth, slowly, slowly.

A collective moan of terror and adoration arose in the broadcast room. Even Zlotny vented a long, keening wail. Only Paterson stood silent, not even watching the monitor. He watched Zlotny, and his hands opened and closed, as though around a throat.

The robed and horned man looked toward Paterson and drew himself together. He came over, smiling blandly again, and made a sweeping gesture. "The camera is yours, Doctor Paterson. But before you speak, would you like to know why I have permitted you to come here? Why I have taken so much trouble to see that you could reach me when the best of my enemies could not?"

Paterson did not speak, but he waited.

"Because, dear Jon Paterson, it is written in the Final Testament that there shall come to the Great Servant one who seeks violence, one who bears a message, one who embodies all the tenets of the Testament." He watched Paterson closely. "It is written, Doctor, that one will come in the last moments who will be a greater servant to the Duality even than I. A person who will be the scourge of the planet, the very embodiment of evil incarnate. And now you are here." He made the gesture of invitation again. "Go, servant Jon Paterson. Speak to the earth. Warn them if you will."

But it was too late. The Lorsii had come.

* * * *

91

BOOK TWO

CHAPTER TEN

The Lorsii came in their bright ships like clouds of jewels tinkling. They came to the nations of Earth and the seas and the deserts. They came on pillars of fire and smoke. They came to gatherings of the soldiers of the Army of the Final Testament, and to some they threw bagsful of jewels and golden images, and to others they gave vast sheets of living flame which struck and stuck and charred. They came to the huddled masses of the disbelievers, the Christians and Muslims and Taoists and atheists, and to some they threw jewels, and to others they gave the fire. But there was no pattern to their giving.

They came to the great pipelines of the Arctic oil fields, and it pleased them to give fire to run down the pipes. They came to the skid rows of Paris and gave jewels, tossed overside from their graceful ships. And as the people scrabbled up the new-found wealth, the Lorsii gave them showers of acid.

They came to the saintly and the depraved, and some among them threw trinkets and some threw bombs wrought in forms of heartrending loveliness. They came among the starving and gave manna which nourished and manna which poisoned.

They came to a city and lifted it bodily off the earth, leaving it suspended in fear and anticipation. They came to another city and caused it to be made flat on the stones.

They came to rivers and burnt them dry. They came to Greenland and caused the ice cap to bubble and boil, sending trillions of tons of water into the oceans to flood the shores half a world away.

And they came to Dos Rios in a ship like a slow-motion swan. They sang a song in their voices like crystal breaking, and the town shattered and crumpled into dust, even as the people crumpled. They sat their ship on the long lake and caused the waters to become blood. They moved on the shores in complex motions which may have been games or communications or rituals. And they flew away without finding the cave.

It was two days before Rebecca Martin lifted the rock which hid the cave's opening. She gagged and retched, but held the rock up. The entire lake, several miles long, was a dark, festering red. Not bloodlike or blood-colored, but bloody. Coagulated and scummed with thousands of dead fish. The very air reeked, and the sky itself was layered with smoke and ashes to the horizons. It looked, she thought, exactly as she'd always imagined hell.

Crick called from the darkness of the cave. "What do you see, child? And what's that smell?"

"I think you'd better come look for yourself, Poppa-Bear."

Crick scrambled up awkwardly and wedged himself into the crevice beside Rebecca. He looked a long time. "God save us," he said softly.

"I think we'd better drop the rock again, Grandpa, or I'm going to be sick all over both of us."

They lowered the stone and slid back down into their rocky sanctuary. Rebecca made tea on a camp stove while Crick stroked his Bible as if for comfort. "The hardest thing, for some reason, is admitting that you and Jon were right," Rebecca said. "I think that all along I believed that any minute you would come to your senses. I thought that knowing the Honeybucket was finished had made you—made you—"

"Crazy. An old loony, gone dotty with religion. Seen lots of 'em in my time, child. Think the Lord's spoken to them direct. You had no reason to believe any different about me."

"But I did, Poppa-Bear. I've been with you all my life, and I know you're sane. You're the sanest man I ever met! I don't know how I could have made myself believe otherwise. I guess I j-just didn't have enough faith." Her voice had gotten small and humble toward the end.

Crick sighed and pushed his glasses up on his forehead. "Well, child, we're all tested. And many folks come to the Lord after lives of terrible sin or great resistance. The Lord has often chosen His best tools from among those who had been His worst enemies."

Rebecca was silent while the tea boiled, and she poured it into the tin cup the two of them were sharing. When she spoke again, her fright was obvious. "Is this really the end of the world, Grandpa? Is this the end of it all?"

Crick accepted the cup and held it gingerly. "I don't know, Becky. Sure looks like it, don't it? But it never pays to second-guess the Creator. When He destroyed Sodom and Gomorrah, many good Christians thought it was Armageddon. And when Jesus died and arose, even some of the disciples thought the Second Coming was right around the corner. Every earthquake and flood was thought to be the end of things. That was better'n two thousand years ago, and we're still here."

"But you believe it's the end, don't you?"

Crick was torn. His granddaughter wanted so desperately to believe that the horror outside was a passing thing, and he wanted so desperately to assure her that it was. But he could not lie to her. "Yes, Becky, I believe it is."

"Are you ready, Grandpa? Can you give up your life right now and face eternity?"

"I am as ready as I have always been, Rebecca."

She buried her face in her hands and sobbed. "I'm not, Poppa-Bear. I want to live! I know it's wrong, and I know I should feel differently, but I can't."

The captain handed her his Bible. "Says in here, Becky, that the Lord created the heavens and the earth in seven days. Couple of other places, it says things about time. Old Reverend Brighton and me once had a discussion on the relativity of time, an' he believed that God's days might be a lot longer than ours. Now, it says that when Noah was on the flood, it rained forty days and forty nights, but whose days and nights? Scientists back in the twentieth century figured out that at one period in the earth's history it rained for seven hundred thousand years!"

The woman had stopped weeping and was listening intently, almost hopefully. "What are you saying, Poppa-Bear?"

"Well, let's suppose it really is Armageddon, the last battle. What makes you think that it's going to be a one-day affair? Lordy, child, God tested the Israelites for forty years! What's to say this battle won't go on for that long—or four hundred?"

She blinked. "I—you know, that's possible, isn't it?"

"Anything's possible, Becky, for God. He never promised us simple solutions, did He? 'Fact, He made it clear that we could never understand Him fully. All we can do, child, is follow His commands and try to interpret His word as best we can." Crick sat the teacup down carefully and turned down the lantern. "Right now, I suggest that we get to sleep. Armageddon or no Armageddon, there's still the

Lord's work to do, and we'll do it better when we're rested."

"Yes, Poppa-Bear," she replied, already pulling her sleeping bag around her shoulders. But the Lord's work was not uppermost in her mind. Her inner vision saw only the stinking, death-laden lake of blood outside, and her heart was filled with dread. She closed her eyes, but sleep was a long time coming, and peopled with nightmares wherein a horned figure stood over her with a bloody knife. At times the figure was Ibrihim Zlotny, and at times it was Jon Paterson.

* * * *

It was a more luxurious cave than the one which held Rebecca Martin and Josiah Crick. It had paneled walls and Maori-modern furniture and massage beds. It had a kitchen which could feed fifty people for two years, and a communications center which could reach half the earth, and seven thousand hours of taped music. It had plasteel doors and air filters and a water recycling system. It even had a small tree and a patch of grass in a box. But it was a cave nonetheless, two hundred meters deep in the bedrock beneath The Hague.

Lars Falstrom, haggard and red-eyed, sat staring at the four television screens built into the wall. Three were blank and the last showed only static. As a man crossed the room behind him, he spoke. "Any word on Armin yet?"

The man stopped. "Yes, Mister President. The Turkish Secretary chose to go home just before the basta—the aliens destroyed The Hague. He died with his family on a road outside Ankara."

"Thank you," Falstrom said heavily. Another light went out on the board in his mind. "Would you see if Charlotte is free, Tom?"

"Yes, Sir."

Charlotte Honesdale came in a minute later, recognizable only by her graceful walk. Her entire head was swathed in bandages, leaving a jack-o'-lantern face of holes for mouth and eyes. "I'm sorry, Lars. I meant to tell you myself, but—"

"Yes, you've been busy. We've got to keep going through the motions, don't we? Must get those directives out, the memos duplicated, the pronouncements pronounced, the—"

"Lars! Mister President!"

Falstrom shuddered and sank deeper into the sofa. "I'm sorry, Charlotte. Thank you."

"We are still the government, Lars."

"That's just it. We *are* the government, we few dozen souls hiding down here."

"There are still officials out there, Lars. There have to be."

"So what? What could they do, even if we could contact them? Should I order them to arrest the aliens? We couldn't even stop Zlotny."

The American woman folded her hands in her lap, as though she were at an afternoon social. The gesture was incongruous and unconscious, but it had an oddly comforting effect on both her and Falstrom. "Lars, there are a lot of people left. Maybe as many as twenty percent of them are not under Zlotny's control. That's close to a hundred million people scattered around the world who are looking to us for guidance; some plan, some action. Even word that we still exist. We can't stop the Lorsii right now, but maybe we can eventually if we start looking for weak spots."

Falstrom pressed the heels of his hands against his eyes and rubbed hard. "All right, Charlotte. You get an 'A' in cheerleading. How are you on practical plans?"

Her smile showed even through the bandages. "I'd flunk, most probably, but we've got to start somewhere."

The president got to his feet, limping badly. "Then, let's make it a good show while it lasts. Get the boys working on a hang-in-there speech for me, and I'll figure a way to get it heard."

* * * *

The breeze was warm and invigorating, lifting his krra with its swirls of ice crystals. His hearts beat faster with the joy of the moment, and he trembled on the delicious edge of ego-death, his spirit hiked up in precarious balance even as the boat hiked up on one razor-edged runner. How thin could he slice the line between life and death, between swift racing flight over the endless frozen plain of joyworld and shattering destruction, skidding before the glitterwind in a tangle of spars and masts, sails and wings, blood and wine? Would poems be written in his name? Would songs be sung to his krra? Would he melt into the small, precious namepool of those whose living and ending were the krra of the race itself? Would his ending be of such beauty as that of the legendary Har-Vakka, who composed songs and poems for three days and nights, as the fire-mites of Shuurll ate out his eyes? Would he pass into history with Kayya-Ky, who turned his krra to every being on a whole planet and died with each of them as he fired the globe?

Or would he, in a laughing, lilting moment, provide an instant's entertainment for those who sailed behind; perhaps a higher comment in its own way than the glories of more vasty deaths?

Ah, but not to taste again the wine, no more to race the glitterwind, no more to mate on the high, sharp crags....

Jnn-Pttrsan eased the sheets and spilled wind from the boat's garnet-studded sail. The boat slammed back down on both its runners with a jolt that blurred his vision. For an instant, the bitter plain was gone and in its place, a room with dark walls and shadowy figures. One moved in front of him and spoke, the voice echoing as though coming from the depths of a well. Asking something, demanding.

"Would'st thou join with us now, Jnn-Pttrsan? Would'st ride the winds of other worlds in the Great Boats?"

He looked at the tall, beautiful figure skating along beside his boat, and his hearts were moved by her grace. Surely no wings had ever been held thus, their very shape a comment on the thirty-sixth form? Surely no body had ever glistened and sheened like this, no thorax ever been so slim, no legs ever so thin and shapely. His voice wanted to cry out but his mouth would not form the words. "I—I— hate you! Let me up. I'll kill you."

She blurred, and the ice with her. In her place was the benign, smiling face of a man whose name he could not remember. A man with horns on his head and something cold and gleaming in his hands. The man nodded. "Perhaps a bit more voltage is called for," he said, like someone testing a soup and recommending salt.

She lifted, her wings a gossamer cloud around her, and his hearts rose with her as she kited off into the sky. He felt himself pulled, up, up, out of the boat, his own wings spreading in the thin, snow-whipped wind. He felt himself arching free of gravity, of thought, of purpose. He was powerful, he was strong. He was one with his krra and one with the creature of light and darkness pirouetting through the vaulted sky ahead of him.

She sang him up the sky with songs of desire and want and need. She recited him to a far, high mountain with poems whose rhythm was heat and whose meter was time. She played him down the wind with musks of her body cast into the currents of the air. And she jeweled him to a snowswept ledge with coy views of her wingroots and the insides of her hands. And she lay herself in postures of submission as he alit beside her, then let herself fall languorously off the ledge in a playful swoon. "Wilt thou be of us and with us, Jnn-Pttrsan? Wilt thou carry the fire of the Great Game?"

And even as he screamed inside, even as he fought for his last hold on sanity, he folded his wings and fell down the face of the mountain after her. "Yes! Oh, yes! I will!"

And he met her in the air and was consumed even as he consumed her.

And sat up on the table and smiled.

In the hot, fetid room, Ibrihim Zlotny stood in his horns and stained scarlet robes, smiling back at him. Half a dozen other people stood or sat in the room. All were dirty, all were disheveled, all were smiling. "Welcome, servant," Zlotny said. "Come, it is time for you to perform your first service, and to receive your first reward." He held out his left hand.

Paterson took it and was led as if he were a child. The others followed: a procession. They went through halls and doorways, and out onto a balcony. Below, a courtyard was filled with Zlotnyites chanting a low, dark song. Cameras turned their glass eyes toward the balcony.

Zlotny lifted his hands for silence. "There comes now he who was spoken of, the Second Servant. He comes to lift the torch which I lay down. My work is finished, his about to begin. Here forward, fellow servants, the Servant Paterson shall be as the Left Hand on Earth."

Paterson stood to one side of Zlotny and slightly behind him. His face showed a radiant suffusion as of unspeakable joy, but his eyes were the eyes of a dead man.

As he stood, hands moved on and around him, robing him in crimson and hanging the cross of the Left Hand about his neck. Deft hands shaved his head while others shaped two locks into horns and pomaded them in place. His own hands hung at his side as if they belonged to someone else.

"Ye faithful," Zlotny cried. "Now are among you the demons of the Left Hand, walking among men on the earth. Ye have seen them; ye have felt their awful breath and heard their mighty mouths speak. Now shall ye know that they are not only among men but *of* them."

He signaled and stepped back from the edge of the balcony, as though to surrender a spotlight.

Paterson was propelled gently forward until he stood against the balcony railing. All eyes looked to a door at the end of the balcony.

Two acolytes opened the door. In the darkness, gleamings and red glitterings showed. A figure stepped out into the sunlight. It was nearly three/meters tall, its feral, triangular head brushing the roof of the balcony. Its multi-faceted eyes reflected the light in sharp-edged splinters, and the lapis lazuli set in its wings were a cloak of cold, blue fire. It moved forward with the quick, scuttling motion of the insectoid, its arms and clawed hands open in a parody of welcome. It clicked when it walked, and it stank.

"Servant Paterson," Zlotny cried, "behold thy bride!"

Jon Paterson stepped forward into the Lorsii's embrace, his own arms open. "Oh, Lord," he said in an emotional voice. "She's so *beautiful!*"

CHAPTER ELEVEN

Bit by bit, information began to trickle into the bunker under The Hague. There appeared to be a fluctuating number of Lorsii vessels, but the average figure was something under a hundred. Lorsii came and went from their ships, and there seemed to be around fifty thousand of them, though no one would swear to that figure. Neither their physical nor linguistic morphology was yielding much of use: they were insectoid—obviously so—but not in any way kin to Terran insects; morphemic analysis of the high-speed chitter they used for communication gave no coherent bases or repetitions. What was the purpose of the sac-like objects beneath their wings? What branch of evolution's tree gave them retractable bony ridges—like skateblades—on the same flattened feet which bore suckers? Why did they have mouths instead of mandibles? And how could such thin, exoskeletal bodies, visibly meant for flight, hold such enormous strength? A Lorsii (Lorsus? Lorsum?) had been observed to pick up a hundred-and-thirty-kilo turbine and carry it to one of the ships with no apparent effort.

Most perplexing and frustrating of all was the question of why they had come and what they were going to do.

"They aren't making sense, Charlotte," Lars Falstrom said. He was sitting in his bed, still in his nightclothes and under the covers. Reports and photographs littered the blankets. An untouched breakfast stood on the sidestand. "I know I'm anthropomorphizing, but they're not behaving like they should."

The American Secretary, her bandages now reduced to a compress on one cheek and another over her eye, sat crosslegged on the floor amid her own clutter of reports. "I know, Lars. They've made no moves to take over in the sense of proclaiming themselves conquerors, and they've established no bases or fortifications. You know what it's like, Lars? It's as if they see us as a huge joke, or a toy to be played with."

"Yes, that's the feeling, isn't it? We're like some ant farm or exhibit. They wander around and use us or ignore us and go back to their ships when it's time for lunch—or whatever; has anybody noticed if they eat?"

"Of course they do, Lars. However alien, they're biologic and living, and they have to eat."

"Perhaps, but nobody's seen any sign that they do anything else biologically necessary. Nobody's seen them have sex, or excrete, or—die."

"If there'd been Martians around back in '98, they would have gotten the same impression of us. We sent strong, male astronauts who ate and excreted and slept in their ships. As far as a Martian could have seen, Earth was populated by blond male Caucasians in their twenties and thirties."

"Okay, I grant you that we may not be seeing the whole picture with them. But they don't act like a scientific group, or a military group, or even a trade group. They've taken no measurements, no samples, no data. They've offered no trades and established no colonies. All they've done is kill and burn and loot."

"Well, they *have* given out jewels."

"But as trade? No, they've tossed them out the way you throw breadcrumbs to pigeons. Only, some of the breadcrumbs are poisoned."

Charlotte stretched full-length along the floor, reaching for a pen. "If they have a salient characteristic, it's their random wantonness. Do we have anybody working on a Lorsii psychological profile?"

"We had Doctor Hardin, up in Alberta, but the zombies got him. A fellow doctor. One of the patients got her later, purely by accident. Poetic justice, I suppose, but we lost Hardin."

"Speaking of the Alberta Facility—or more accurately, one of its inmates—have you heard about Paterson?"

Falstrom's face showed disgust. "Yes, I watched his 'wedding.' Do you think he was a Zlotnyite all along, Charlotte?"

"No, I think they got to him."

"Yeah, and now he's getting to us. They're touring him all over the world, you know. Him and his ravishing bride."

"I don't understand that, either. They've proven we're helpless. They don't need to rub it in."

The president slid out of bed and reached for his jumper. "Maybe they do. With the power they have, they didn't need Zlotny, either, but they used him to soften us up. Maybe they're not quite as invincible as they'd like us to think, uh?"

"Maybe, but that might be a dead end, Lars. I think the psychological angle is the right track." She got up and began gathering her scattered papers. "Suppose you work on the chink-in-the-armor idea and I'll get on the psychology?"

"Fair enough. And Charlotte?"

"Yes?"

"I'd wear a gun. McNally, over in cryptography, went zombie a little while ago."

The tall woman looked pained. "Even Jim? Next thing you know, you and I will be looking at each other suspiciously."

The president reached beneath his jumper's waist and extracted a small laserpistol. "I do, Charlotte."

* * * *

"I wonder where the Honeybucket is now, Poppa-Bear?"

Crick looked up from his book, nearly losing his balance and falling off the skinny mule he was riding. "Abandoned, most likely, Becky."

"You don't think the Zlotnyites have dismantled her do you, or burned her?"

"I doubt it. They seem to have no interest in anything involving cooperative effort. Since Doctor Paterson got through, I think it likely that they just left the *Milk & Honey* wherever he got out of her."

Rebecca, walking along holding the mule's lead rope, muttered something beneath her breath.

"Beg pardon, child?"

"*We* did it, Grandpa! We brought that monster down from Canada and delivered him like a pizza."

"Now, Becky. Remember that Jon is not moving at his own will. He's—"

"He's become Zlotny, that's what he's done. We should have ground him into the ice when we had the chance." She looked around guiltily. Her voice had risen, and the people nearest them in the stream of refugees on the road were watching her curiously and resentfully. Among the new set of unwritten laws which had taken hold with the coming of the Lorsii was one which stated that people should speak in whispers, move with caution, keep the head down. Overnight, the race had adopted a posture of humiliation. It had turned to watching the ground before its feet, as if unable or unwilling to raise its eyes to the destruction and evil through which it moved. Anyone who showed feeling, who spoke loudly, who was not cowed and beaten, was regarded as either a zombie or a zombie sympathizer.

Rebecca glared around her defiantly, but lowered her voice. "I can't keep up with you, Josiah. Sometimes you talk as if you think Paterson was crazy, and sometimes as if he were sane. Sometimes you sound like he's a poor, misguided nut and other times you sound like he's an Angel of the Lord. And no matter what he does—steal your ship or become a front for the bugs—you say it's all according to plan and you forgive him."

Crick clucked the mule to a halt and let his granddaughter help him dismount. He sat himself on a rock beside the road and got out his Bible. "I don't really know if Jon's crazy, Becky, and I don't believe it matters. But I do know that the Lord has plans for him, as He has for you and me and everyone else that's left on Earth." He opened the book.

"As to forgiving him, that's not my place—or yours." He indicated the skinny mule. "Suppose our patient friend here were to bite you? Would you forgive him?"

"Poppa-Bear, that's an animal. He doesn't know better."

"So you'd forgive him."

"Yes."

"Now, let's suppose he somehow acquired a mind. He could think. And he bit you again."

She thought about it. "I wouldn't forgive him."

Crick beamed; the same look he got when he had maneuvered the young woman into a trap at chess. "Ah, but intelligence does not imply morality. Would you forgive an intelligent cannibal his eating habits, if he had not been shown the Grace of God?"

She sighed. "All right, Josiah. It's the morality that counts. If the mule knew right from wrong and bit me, I'd have grounds for not forgiving him. But Paterson's not a mule, and he knows right from wrong."

"What if the mule here had all those qualities, was a practicing Christian—" he smiled at her look of outrage—"was a practicing Christian, I say, and was suddenly stricken by mental illness."

Rebecca Martin's mouth opened and closed twice. She kicked at pebbles angrily. "Then we're back to the original mule."

"For all practical purposes." Crick sighted down his nose and through his glasses. "But you're missing the real point, Becky. Even if the mule were consciously evil, as you feel Jon Paterson is, it is not yours to judge."

"Oh, yeah? Well, the Bible has a lot to say about casting out evil, and about fighting it."

"That is true. But your feelings toward Jon Paterson are not the righteous wrath of the believer. They are the wounds of a woman in love."

"What! Josiah Crick, how *dare* you insinuate—"

"Our problem," Crick went on, his face in his Bible to hide the smile on his lips, "is not Jon Paterson and the path he is taking, but ourselves and the path the Lord wants us to take. The battle is still on, child, and there is work to be done. We must gather our forces and find how God wants us to combat this infestation of demons which has come upon us."

Rebecca Martin was red and flushed, her eyes flashing. She turned to the mule and stopped in midstride. All around them, refugees had halted, until now there was a semicircle of perhaps sixty people watching her and Crick. "What do *you* want?" she snarled. "Go on, let us alone."

A man with a child on his hip stepped forward, facing Crick rather than the girl. He cleared his throat apologetically. "Excuse me, brother. Did I hear you say that you're a Christian?"

Crick nodded. "I am."

"So are we. We're interested in what you said about the Lord's wanting us to fight."

* * * *

Kojja-Je entered the private sphere of his wingmate and immediately folded himself into the cone of nonpresence, his wings furled around his body to present nothing more than his jeweled beauty, should his intrusion accidentally disturb her and cause her to look his way. He tried for the nineteenth form, *respectful submission while awaiting attention,* knowing its very difficulty would be a comment should he fail perfection of pose or odor. He watched her through the tawny translucence of his wing membrane, marveling as always at the perfection of her concentration.

She sat on a Beeppu board suspended over the gulf of air, her wings bound with the thirty-knot cord. The board pivoted on the graceful rail of the boat's flight platform, its inboard end weighted with a block of either/or ice whose melting was erratic and beyond calculation. Already it teetered, dipping her toward the clouds below and the death below them.

A skreee away, bound members of the planet's soft, ugly

populace waited their turn, each radiating odors and sounds of fear. One by one they were brought forward to stare into Kojja-Je's wingmate's eyes, that she might drink of their minds and emotions, and one by one they were cast over the side that she might share the ecstasy of their dying.

The last one went shrieking down through the air, and she sat savoring, her posture utterly controlled. Not a flicker of movement, not a waft of odor betrayed the receptiveness of her *krra*. Even when the either/or ice shed a sudden burst of weight and tipped the Beeppu board perilously, she did not move.

Finally, she looked toward the platform. Kojja-Je and her two handmaidens displayed the hundred-and-ninth form, *applause and intense admiration.*

"Dost thou love me, Kojja-Je?" she asked.

"As the winds of joyworld, Hass-Ka-Ve."

"Lovest me thirty knots worth?"

His *krra* lifted as death blew through the platform. "Even though bound myself."

She odored satisfaction and acceptance to him and signaled to have the board drawn in. "I believe thee, and this time shall not put thee to the test."

"To drink the wine," he said, relieved.

"To feel the wind," she replied as the handmaidens unbound her. "It is said that when Mxxu-Be-Twe chose to fall, her lover untied the thirty knots, and after freeing her, chose to fall himself."

"A poetic comment." He groomed her wings as she shook the wrinkles out of them. "I trust your *krra* was lifted by the sharing of those deaths."

"Not a great deal. They are a crude and insensitive race. There was not a song or poem among them, though in some a calling upon something larger and a kind of peace at the end."

"How novel. Shall we fly?"

"No. I find the air here as oppressive as the people. Let us to wine instead."

"To wine, then."

They skated the convoluted passages of the Great Boat, their movements a comment on movement. Here and there they passed openings into niches and compartments, rooms and emptiness. In some were Lorsii; in others, objects; and in still others, humans and their artifacts. Screams came from some places, and passing Lorsii made the sixtieth form, *momentary appreciation tempered with other commitments.* In one room, a man was spreadeagled in midair, apparently encased in transparent slime which was connected by mucus-like strands to the walls of the compartment. It was Jon

Paterson.

"Thy toy, Hass-Ka-Ve; does it continue to amuse thee?"

She paused, watching Paterson writhe slowly in the glutinous mass holding him. "This one alone has a poem, though it is a dull and turgid one. This Jnn Pttrsan could have been an egg of the Great People, had he been born to us. He is as a Mffa-Le among Dtte-Kkomm."

Kojja-Je felt an odor almost of jealousy, and for an instant retreated into the two-hundredth form, *passing interest*, to enjoy it and share it with his wingmate. "But a Mffa-Le is still a lower form, joy of my nostrils, and thou art a Lorsii."

She emanated the sixteenth courting form, *coy amusement*. "Dids't attend our nuptials, wingmate? And their consummation?"

"It amused me not to," Kojja-Je said, trying to waft tolerant dignity toward her. "Thou didst not truly mate with the beast?"

Her laughter was as fine things shattering. " 'Twould be a fine new sensation! But nay, pride of my wings. 'Twas not anatomically possible." She postured the double-entendre form, *but if it were....*"Come, the wine, the wine!"

* * * *

CHAPTER TWELVE

Ibrihim Zlotny knelt before the bloodstained altar, his encarnadined hands clasped before him. A wet smear of blood led from the altar to the curtained door at one side of the dark room, and the sound of something inert being dragged along could still be heard through the curtains. A pentagram was chalked on the floor, its lines now smudged and broken. On the altar stood a lightning-slashed, horned cross, and on the wall behind it a hologram of the goat-hooved Great Enemy, his arms around two Lorsii. Zlotny's eyes were on the hologram.

"Master," he said, his voice low and filled with adoration. "I have served you well. I have prepared my people for the coming of your demons. I have been your Judas-goat and led them to your presence. I have done all that you have asked of me, even to stepping aside for your Servant, Paterson. I am now as the lowest of your followers. You have taken me to the heights and cast me down again, even as your symbol the serpent." He bowed his head to the floor and pressed it into the pentagram.

"For you, master, I have forsaken home and family. I have turned from the half-path of the Right Hand, though my father's fathers followed the Way of Jesus since time untold."

He raised up, his hands on his knees, and stared at the hologram, and his look held the slightest bit of defiance. "All this have I done for you, master, that you should fulfill your promise to me: that like the Servant of the Right Hand, Moses, I should pass not through the flame but should come alive into your kingdom; that I should fly in the Great Boats to the very stars; that I should taste the wines unknown to mere mortals; that I—" his eyes dropped, and his voice shook. "That I should live forever."

He raised his eyes again, a look almost of pleading in them now. "When shall I know my reward, master? When shall the hosts call me in song and beauty, to rise in the air and fly away with you? Why have you taken your voice from me, now that my work for you is done?"

He waited for the ringing in his ears, the floating away, the haloed vision which always preceded a command from the master. He waited, wondering how long it would be before the millions who still bowed to him realized that he no longer held power, that his transfer of authority to Jon Paterson had been the last act he had performed which had the might of the Lorsii behind it. He waited, there on his knees in growing fear. And waited....

* * * *

Josiah Crick was asleep when Rebecca came into the tent, but he woke instantly. "Yes, child?"

"Grandpa, there's a large group of zombies about three klicks down the hill. They're burning as they come."

Crick rolled painfully out of his blanket, shooing Hezekiah and Beelzebub off his stomach. "No chance that they'll pass us unseen?"

"Poppa-Bear, we've got three hundred people up here and a third of them are children. Some baby's bound to cry, or someone's bound to kick something over."

"Yes, I suppose that's so." He fumbled in the darkness for his coat; the night was chill. "What are the people doing?"

"Waiting for you, Grandpa." There was a resonance of pride in her voice.

Crick dressed himself slowly, but his mind was moving at top speed. Conflicting emotions coursed through it, and he felt like a blind man with his hands out, seeking obstacles which he could not see. What would God have of him? What should he do about the three hundred souls now cowering on the frosty mountainside? And why should it be he, a bent and used-up sailor, to whom these people looked for decisions? Hadn't he done enough, giving them the comfort of the Word? Was his business not with Ibrihim Zlotny? And why had he accepted the mantle of leadership in the first place? He'd seen it coming, back on the highway; he'd commanded too many 'liners and crews not to recognize the symptoms.

As he pulled his coat around his shivering shoulders, he heard the first, distant sounds of the oncoming mob, raucous and discordant like a flock of crows, punctuated by the stutters of firecrackers or guns and occasional screams.

He stepped out of the tent and stood up in the moonlight. "Becky, where's my cane?"

"I don't know, Grandpa. It's around here somewhere."

A woman stepped out of the shadows. "Here, Josiah. Use this." She handed him a knobby tree limb, taller than he was.

"Thank you," Crick said, aware of the symbolism, and aware at that moment of the image he must present, standing on the rise in his flowing coat and flowing beard, a staff in his hand. Is this Thy doing, he asked in his mind, or just the melodrama of an old man?

But whether it was the Lord's will or his own fancy, to the frightened people gathering around him, Crick knew that he looked the patriarch. He knew, too, that at this moment and this place, a patriarch was needed, even one who couldn't read his Bible without glasses. He squared his shoulders and raised the staff. "Children of the Lord," he cried. "What would you have of me?"

The man who had first stopped on the road came forward. "Father Josiah," he said, as if testing the sound. It was the first time Crick had been addressed that way.

Crick felt something descend on him, something warm and strong and comforting. He wanted to throw himself on the ground in trembling fear and worship. But the Presence which was upon him put a strength in his limbs. As he regarded the man before him, Crick's face displayed wisdom. "Yes, my son?" And with that acceptance, the mantle was upon him.

"Father Josiah, what are we to do? We cannot flee with all our children, and we have no weapons to stand and fight."

Josiah lifted his face to heaven, and the moonlight shone on his long beard. His eyes were closed. "The prophet Joel said, 'Like chargers they gallop on. The country is like a garden of Eden ahead of them and a desert waste behind. At sight of them the peoples are appalled and every face grows pale.'"

He opened his eyes and looked over the huddled Christians. "Throughout the history of the world, God's enemies have come upon us with war and the sword. And we have usually been unarmed and unprepared.

"Yet, have the good not won more battles than the evil? Do we not have God's word that good will always triumph?" A murmured agreement came to him. "Then, Brothers and Sisters, let us cast aside our fears and doubts. Let us gird ourselves in the armor of God. Let us stand as men and Christians and trust in the Lord to deliver our enemies unto us."

People were standing straighter. A few men picked up rocks or branches, hefting them experimentally.

Josiah strode forward, his arms outflung and his staff held high. "Come, let us prepare a reception for the ungodly—one such as shall make them fear the name of the Lord and the arm of his servants!"

In ones and twos at first, then in a mass, they followed Josiah down the mountainside toward the advancing minions of Ibrihim Zlotny.

* * * *

The swanboat fell gracefully from the belly of the Great Boat, wafting down like a leaf on an autumn wind. The island below was a topaz set in a sea of emerald, and on the beaches where the one met the other, an edge of obsidian separated them. The obsidian was like peppercorns to the eye: thousands upon thousands of uniformed soldiers of the Army of the Final Testament.

As the boat descended, its flaming wings opened flat, and there was a throne upon its back. Jon Paterson sprawled indolently across the throne, and beside him was Hass-Ka-Ve, her own wings opened to precisely the same angle as the boat's: the fifty-fourth form, *unity with all that we have made.*

The boat touched the sea, and the waters boiled around it. Thousands of Zlotnyites waded out, their hands transfixed in the mutant-cross salute and their faces shining. They waded into the boiling waters and did not appear to notice that the flesh was cooking off their bones. They smiled and mouthed shouts of welcome as they boiled away and sank. And others took their places until the sea cooled and the sides of the boat were black with worshipers.

Jon Paterson waved to the throng listlessly, as though acknowledging a gift of no worth. He smiled at the soldiers, though the smile was a rictus. Through clenched teeth, he tried to shout, to scream, to curse.

Beside him, Hass-Ka-Ve stroked his thigh with her alien, hard-shelled fingers. Her *krra* was lifted by his hatred, his struggle. She let the mingling of his hatred and the mindless adoration of the crowd wash through her, a comment on the power of the individual *krra.* Here was one being, one unit of such intensity that the *beat, beat, beat* of his *krra* bore down on and overpowered the whole throb of the crowd. She set her hands and head into the seventieth form, *respectful acknowledgment of superior quality in an inferior being,* and she meant it.

For the gathered crowd, she made the courting and submission forms in her language, causing Jon Paterson to rise from the throne and jerk through the motions with her. Then she made the same motions in his language: turning her head from his embrace, then submitting; covering her thorax and abdomen against his questing hands, then submitting; laying herself back in the odd postures required by his race. And all the while, the soldiers of the Army chanted and applauded, some giving in to a copulative frenzy of their own.

And when it was finished, the swanboat rose in the air, burning all beneath into ashes and grease bubbling on the salt sea.

On the veranda of a fine house overlooking the beach and village, a grey-haired woman clutched a small gold cross to her bosom and cried. Both her sons and her only daughter had been in the water around the swanboat.

The belly of the Great Boat opened and swallowed the swanboat. In the lightened gravity which prevailed inside the ship, Hass-Ka-Ve unfurled her wings and flew in a lazy circle around the throne. "Rise now, Jnn-Pttrsan," she cried in her brittle, uninflected voice. "I drink your *krra*. Now you speak me your hate, yes?"

Paterson stood up like a lame man, shaking and unsteady. He spat toward the Lorsii as she drifted by him. "I'll give you hate. You and the rest of your murdering friends."

Hass-Ka-Ve landed in a difficult pirouette, momentarily sad that none were there to see the near perfection of the motion. "What means friend, Jnn-Pttrsan?" She appeared relaxed, her odor one of calm and contemplation. But the aura around the earthman, running into the ultraviolet, told her he was about to spring at her, and she delighted in the subtlety of her pose, for its relaxation masked a two-form change into flight-with-grace-and-speed. "Friend new word me."

"A friend," Paterson said, tensing, "is someone who—" he sprang, his fingers clawing.

She lifted and came down near the edge of the still-open landing platform. "Friend is to share, like wine?"

Paterson lay there, trembling with rage and humiliation. "Yeah, friend is to share, like wine." He started to rise, but was stopped by a touch of her foot. He saw her head tilted in an oddly human gesture of query.

"Tell me about 'friend,' Jnn-Pttrsan."

"You damn sure aren't *my* friend," he answered hotly. "Nor any earthman's. Friends help each other. You're an enemy, a monster."

"I help wingmate, help Great People. This make me friend?"

Paterson nodded grudgingly. "Yeah, I guess that makes you a friend to them. Even Hitler had friends, I guess."

"What means 'Hitler'?"

Paterson's laugh was nasty. "He's a guy you'd've liked. He butchered and murdered and killed, just like you people. He was evil."

"What means 'evil'?"

"Oh, hell! Evil means what you're doing is—" Paterson's vision blurred. There was a horrible moment of *deja vu*. Hadn't he had this conversation before? Wasn't he going to have it again, on some frozen plain? His sense of time became confused. He dragged himself mentally back to the Great Boat. "—is wrong."

Hass-Ka-Ve looked out the landing platform at the tops of the clouds drifting below. "Where learn about this 'wrong,' this 'evil'?"

Hass-Ka-Ve made the form for *negligent interest to pass time.* "Know good. Good is to lift *krra*. Good is fierce mating, sharp wine, glitterwind in wires, share life, death with other. But not know evil. What concept this?"

Paterson had walked idly away from the opening and was maneuvering himself toward a lump of what looked like ice or crystal a few meters away from the Lorsii. He shrugged, fondling the lump with feigned disinterest. "Evil is what you're doing to my people below. What you're doing to me."

Hass-Ka-Ve came languorously off the crag-rest and skated over to the opening, her wings moving as if under water in a form peculiar to the females of her race. She gave no apparent notice of Paterson's preoccupation with the lump, nor of his being behind her. At the opening, she trailed her wingtips behind her like a bride's train. "You not enjoy Great Game?"

"Game? You think it's a game to kill people?" The singing was in his ears again. There was a helpless, hopeless terror of the recurrent dream replaying endlessly, each time slightly closer to the final reality of the icy, bloody sunned world and the boats coming after on their spiderleg runners. He lifted the lump and moved quietly toward the Lorsii. "You think those people enjoy being killed? You think *you'd* enjoy dying?"

"Yes. That greatest comment. Lift *krra* of whole race." She turned just as Paterson lifted the lump over his head. She was immobile, calm. "You kill me now, Pttrsan? You kill me as Great People kill your people? What make you different from us?"

The lump wavered. Paterson sweated. "We don't kill for fun, monster. We don't go looking for other planets just so we can turn them into cinders. We kill to protect ourselves."

"Your *krra* say you kill me for hate. This not evil?"

Paterson sagged a little. "Maybe. Maybe. But—I don't know." He lowered the lump. "We're taught it's wrong to kill in hatred."

"Who teach? Curious concept, not kill. Want to meet beast who teach."

"You're too late. He's been here and gone."

"Leave picture? Words? Odor? Instructions?"

"Yeah. The Bible. It's a book. *The* book."

"Where find Bible?"

Paterson weighed his emotions in his head. He replayed the thundering sermons of his childhood, the admonitions against taking vengeance in his own hands. And the other part of him, the scientist and man and human, replayed the horrors of the past days and weeks, the terrible suffering and agony of his people and world. And he made his decision. "There," he said, his voice strained. "Below."

Hass-Ka-Ve's eyes followed his gesturing hand. She looked through the opening.

And Paterson raised the lump and swung. Even as the lump whistled forward, he saw too late that he was standing on her trailing wingtips. She moved ever so slightly, and the wingtips jerked Paterson's feet from beneath him. He fell through the opening toward the Pacific, far, far below.

Hass-Ka-Ve peered over the edge and watched Paterson's dwindling fall, her *krra* vibrating with joy.

"Thou, guardian of my nest." Kojja-Je stood beside her.

"Thou, fire in my ice." She shifted form to *intensely sharing*. "Thy love?"

"As the suns and moons for thee."

"Would'st prove it? Now?"

"My life?"

"No. Not just yet. Would'st fetch for me?"

"The jewel at the heart of the world."

"Again, not this time. I would have a thing called book. Called Bible."

"Done this moment," he said, lifting his wings.

"And one other—"

"Thou?"

"I have lost a toy overside."

Kojja-Je's glands rushed ahead of his control. The odor of intense jealousy came off him.

"Yes," Hass-Ka-Ve said casually. "That toy. Swiftly now, my mate, lest thy speed prove not sufficient." She folded herself into the form for lovers, called *trust with reservations*.

Kojja-Je gathered himself. "Thy toy, or my life." His form was not perfect, for it was one used very seldom and never practiced. *This for thee, and my price shall be terrible.*

He lifted through the opening and beat downward, diving like a meteor toward the glittering waters.

CHAPTER THIRTEEN

Charlotte Honesdale peered cautiously out the broken window at the street below. She took care not to expose more of herself than she had to, and her finger stayed on the trigger of her laser rifle. Nothing moved in the rubble below, but she knew they were out there: smoke still rose from the spot, a kilometer away toward the harbor, where the WorldGov bunker had been.

There was the merest flick of motion at the side of her eye. Something shifted behind an overturned steamer halfway up the block. Charlotte whipped up and out, aiming even as she pulled the trigger. A sear of green light leapt from the rifle to the car, answered instantly by the flash of a projectile gun. Mortar and brickchips stung her face as the bullet creased the edge of the window and slammed into the wall at the back of the room. She dropped back inside, wondering if she'd gotten her opponent, and waited for the yellow "ready" light to go on again in her rifle.

An old gentleman came into the room, almost crawling to keep himself below the window. "The President would like to see you, Madame Secretary. I shall man your emplacement."

Charlotte handed the old man her rifle, smiling at his courtliness. He had been a diplomat a long time. "Thank you, Mister Ambassador. Watch that overturned car up the block."

"You would not know it now, Madame Honesdale, but I was a sharpshooter during the Second War of Incorporation. Did for my share, too."

"I can believe that," she replied. "You've always been a tough old buzzard, Charlie."

The ambassador grew an inch taller and twenty years younger. "You scoot along to the President, Madame, and I shall mind the store."

She threaded her way through the piled supplies and equipment, the loopholed walls and casements, and went down into the basement of the warehouse which was now the last place on Earth flying the flag of the United Governments. She could not help marveling and feeling proud that even under the pressure of losing the bunker battle, of moving to this dilapidated building under fire, the government still continued to function. Information came in and went out by runner, by wire, by television. Men and women operated radios and encoders, analyzer computers and kitchens, sick bays and sandwich wagons while shells thumped into the walls and the world continued to cave in around them.

And Lars Falstrom, when she reached him, was the center of a small whirlwind of activity, himself moving faster than anyone around him. After his initial funk, he had drawn upon the inner reserve which had made him president in the first place, and was driving the ship of state with all sails to the storm and his cannon run out. He looked, Charlotte thought with admiration, like the captain he was.

"Ha, Charlotte," he called. "Come here. I've got some good news for a change—have you eaten yet?—page, bring the Secretary a sandwich—look at this."

"Wait, Lars. Whoa!"

Falstrom grinned and pulled Honesdale down beside him on an overturned ammo case. "Do you know where the center of the universe is?"

"Not without looking in the encyclopedia."

"It's in Alberta, Canada. I used to think it was wherever I happened to be, but no more."

The woman sat nodding, letting him run it out his way.

"First we had Lee Hardin, who had the foresight to let Jon Paterson work, and that gave us the crazy angle. Then we had Paterson himself, who's been grabbed by the bugs. Now guess what we've got?" Without waiting for an answer, he waved a typed report at her. "We've got that old guy who picked Paterson out of the pea-patch, so to speak: Captain Crick. Seems he's turned himself into the whole Old Testament rolled into one and is rallying Christians against both the zombies and the Lorsii." He shook his head as if amazed. "The three key figures in this whole thing, all coming out of an insane asylum in nowhere, Canada."

Charlotte accepted the sandwich the page handed her and munched it thoughtfully. "What's the difference between Crick and the hundreds of other religious leaders who've tried to turn the tide? Epari Subba Rao rallied nearly a million Hindus two weeks after the bugs came, and they were all killed in one night."

Falstrom's grin was wolfish. "A few nights ago, Crick led three hundred unarmed people—half of them kids—down a mountain in Missouri to face a mob of six thousand zombies armed with guns and dynamite. He climbed up on a rock, pointed his staff at the mob, and what do you think happened?"

"Something nasty, I hope."

"Something nasty, indeed. Charlotte, I've got this from five separate eyewitness accounts. Crick pointed his staff, and lightning struck! Hundreds of bolts, out of a crystal-clear sky. It struck down almost a thousand of the zombies, and the rest ran off as fast as their drunken little legs could carry them!"

Charlotte stopped in mid-bite, the sandwich dangling ludicrously from between her lips. She removed it slowly and swallowed without chewing. "You're serious?"

"Yes."

"Couldn't be some Lorsii move, huh? They're pretty good at that kind of wantonness."

"I don't think so. Thus far, no matter how astounding their parlor tricks, they've had to be there to do them. And there wasn't a bug or a bugship in sight."

"Then, what do you think happened?"

Falstrom shrugged. "I'll avoid that question for now. But I know one thing that's happened for certain: the people of Earth have a rallying point and their first clear-cut victory over the zombies. And I'm making sure that the word gets around, you'd better believe!"

"Yes, but what happens when—or rather, if—Crick attracts the attention of the Lorsii? I don't think we can count on lightning striking twice, but we can damn sure count on the Lorsii striking him down."

"We'll cross that bridge if, and I emphasize 'if,' we come to it. Meanwhile, let's make all the hay we can out of lightning striking once." He bounced up. "We're also beginning to get a picture of how the bug mind works. Not much of one, yet, but a little. I want to start getting that information out to people like Crick, in case it can help them. Do you think you could find time to set up a courier system for this stuff?"

"Of course," she said, rising and licking her fingers. "I'll get at it right away." She left immediately, her mind in turmoil. This was the first ray of hope since Zlotny had surfaced, and it was such a tiny one. So many others like it had flared briefly and flickered out. She could not help but think of the comparisons involved. The original problem had been a pseudo-religious zealot, after whom the government had sent a pseudo-madman. Now, the madman was real, and so were his nightmares, and the only hope of the world lay in a real religious zealot. And what of Ibrihim Zlotny himself? Why had he stepped down in favor of Jon Paterson? What were his plans now—or the Lorsii's plans for him?

And most of all, the turmoil in Charlotte Honesdale's mind revolved around a tiny, nagging question that refused to go away. What if it weren't a freak natural accident that had brought the lightning down on Zlotny's zombies? Just in passing, she tried to remember the last time she had prayed, but it escaped her.

* * * *

"I say we attack them now," the woman cried angrily, shaking her fist.

"And I say we let them go in peace. We've our own road to take."

The two speakers glared at each other across the clearing, and behind them, the circle of listeners looked from one to the other with expressions varying from hope to disagreement. Both speakers, and many of the audience, wore the white tunic and rough robe which was quickly becoming emblematic of the group. Every breast, even those of the newborn, bore a cross on a thong. A few were finely wrought pieces of jewelry from before the invasion, but most were rough and wooden, carved or lashed, many made from the boards of desecrated churches the group had passed in its eastward exodus.

The angry woman waved her rifle dramatically northward, where the gutted hulk of the Atlanta IndustriPlex raised its broken skyline above the trees. "Have we come so far to be stopped by fear? Has not the Lord God stood by us? Did He not slay our enemies in Cape Giraudoux, in Natchez, in Birmingham? Do you think He will fail us here?"

A cry of agreement rose from the Christians.

The other speaker waited for silence, then spoke. "Our enemies in those places were men. There are Lorsii yonder."

The cry of agreement which rose was more subdued, but more powerful for that.

The militant woman saw that she was losing the crowd. "It must come sooner or later, Brothers and Sisters. We shall never hold our heads up again until we have faced and conquered that hideous race of demons. And I say we start now!"

The crowd was uncertain. Yeas and nays mingled, and a

shuffling went through the people. Almost by unspoken accord, all heads turned to Josiah, who stood with his hand gently stroking the neck of his skinny mule. His head was down and his long grey beard lay on his robe like a quilt. He held his knotty staff against his cheek and seemed to be asleep as he stood there. Rebecca Martin, on the mule, had her hand on her grandfather's shoulder. She made no move to disturb him.

After a time, he looked up and swept the gathering with his eyes. "We have come a distance," he said, and his voice had grown deeper over the weeks. "We have a distance to go. Let us bear in mind that we are God's creatures, and His servants, and that those who skulk in the ruins of that city there are God's children also." He pointed skyward with his staff. "Even so are those who sail above us, the scourge with which God lashes us." He loosed the mule and strode out into the clearing, his beard and robe flapping in the light wind. "We have not yet *sought* battle with the servants of Satan. When we have fought, it has been in defense." He faced the militant woman. "Now you would take war to the despoilers. Do you do this in God's name, or in your own anger?"

Throughout the crowd, heads dropped in shame.

"I have called upon the Lord each time we have faced peril, and He has answered. Never have I said, 'God of my fathers, slay mine enemies!' I have said, 'Lord, if it be Thy will, deliver us.' "

A little girl raised her hand tentatively. "Father Josiah, Mommy said the *doctor* delivered *me*."

For a moment, there was silence, then a ripple of laughter. The ripple swelled into a roar, with Josiah leading it. He held out his arms for the child and swept her up. "Bless you, little one, so she did. And God was there, too, just as you've shown Him to be here." He held the girl aloft, as if to display her to the gathering. "From out of the mouths of babes!" He sat her down and shooed her toward her mother, then spoke again. "Innocence is God's grace. Let us not sully that any farther than we have to. There will be fighting enough before the battle is over, but for now, let us seek peace." He looked to the east. "Let us away to the mountains, there to build a fastness and a strength in the Lord."

Suiting the action to the words, Father Josiah struck out eastward, and eleven thousand people followed him.

* * * *

Kojja-Je regarded Paterson, swinging below in a netting of mucoid nourishment-web, with a loathing he could not entirely conceal. His glands were in control and he odored nothing more than

121

bland interest, but the tips of his wings were out of alignment, and the relationship of his posture to the dominant lines of the room was positively graceless. He knew this, and knew Hass-Ka-Ve knew he knew, but it didn't matter. He could not understand how such a soft, sluglike creature, a being without the sensitivity even to feel the forms, could attract his wingmate. The Jnn-Pttrsan had not even beauty, had not even mind! Kojja-Je was aware that most of his wingmate's interest was amusement, and that it was her comment to make him thus jealous of so despicable a beast. But he was also aware of a deeper, more serious interest. There was something about this disgusting alien, this slug with its flesh on the outside, which actually attracted her.

"Thou," she asked, her form adding *query thy thoughts discreetly.*

"My labors," he lied, taking the form which said *important matters blur my krra.* "The Grand Admiral grows weary of this dustmote and calls council to determine if we shall have the Great Game here or leave the place for another time."

Hass-Ka-Ve took the second form, *tempered innocence.* "His weariness would have nothing to do with this odd new force the hmmnns have?"

Kojja-Je odored startled surprise. "Thou!"

"Nay, ruby of my hearts. Mine eggmate chanced upon a song of worry, sung by the Grand Admiral's concubine."

"And what did the song sing?"

"Of a man who calls lightnings on the heads of the followers of our fool below, Zlltnnee."

Kojja-Je odored humor, but postured concern. "Rumor, nothing more." Impatience cost him his last grace, and his eighth form bow, *polite request to leave,* was as clumsy as an eggling's. "I leave thee to thy amusements and thy toy."

"To the Grand Admiral with Thee, then?"

"Nay, to wine," he lied again. He turned and very nearly hurried out of her presence.

Hass-Ka-Ve looked for a moment at Paterson, thinking perhaps a poem. But Kojja-Je's crudeness had befouled the room, and she took herself out of it before her *krra* became dulled.

Jon Paterson's eyes snapped open, alert and filled with cunning. For once, he'd come fully awake before they could load his mind up with their drugs and projections. He'd come to consciousness in the web as the two Lorsii had entered the room, brought awake by the wash of their emotions and some strange quirk of time: a feeling that his original nightmare was the key to everything. He swayed now in his sustaining prison of life-jell and savored the secret he'd kept from his captors for nearly a week: that their constant injections and probings at his mind and will had a side effect; he could now understand them in their own tongue. Not perfectly, but well enough. Now, he knew a little about them, about where they came from and what they were doing. And he knew, with a rush of fierce happiness, that the Lorsii were going to lose! He had heard Kojja-Je, had smelt the fear coming off him, knew its cause. Somewhere on the ravaged planet below was the old man in Paterson's original nightmare, the grey-bearded ancient who would turn the key that would unlock the door to the defeat of the Lorsii. And Jon Paterson had not the slightest doubt of that old man's identity.

Quietly, he began to test his bonds.

* * * *

CHAPTER FOURTEEN

It went out by messenger, sometimes carried in hollow legs or sewn into the linings of jackets and jumpers. It went out by wire, radiating out even as the wires were cut behind it. It went out over shortwave transmitters and television, and in spite of the jamming, it occasionally got through. And here and there, in tiny enclaves where the government had held control or regained it, it went out clearly and openly. Josiah Crick—Father Josiah—was winning. Tattered posters with his picture appeared on the sides of gutted buildings, on palm trees, on abandoned vehicles, even pinned to the bodies of dead zombies. The message was in English and Urdu, German and Japanese, Russian and Roukla, Swahili and Senegalese. "God With Us," it proclaimed.

Christians read it in caves and fortified houses, in hideouts and mountaintops. Muslims read it in tents and bazaars. Shinto priests read it beneath their beautiful bronze gongs. Three Bears Running read it to the still-unconquered Apache in the Superstition Mountains. All over Earth, people who held fast to faith read WorldGov's message, and their hearts lifted. In family groups and in ones and twos, they began to trek toward the Appalachian Mountains. For some it was a twenty-thousand-kilometer journey.

Here and there, as the Zlotnyites tore down the posters or ripped out the wires or smashed the television sets, one among them would surreptitiously fold a tattered image and stuff it quickly in his or her boot or jumper. Later, in the dark of privacy, the message

124

would be read and read again. And here and there, a zombie would step out of the black and silver uniform, would pull cap or scarf over the horned head, and would slip away into the night.

The message came to Manitou Springs, carried as a flapping poster on the autumn wind. The NASA complex, like the city around it, was a ghost, for like all despoilers before them, the zombies consumed but did not produce and were forced to move on when they had exhausted the bounty of a place. Now, Manitou Springs was the abode of rats and cockroaches and their two-legged counterparts, those too debauched or too debased even to leave.

And one other. In the complex, the large room which had been turned into Satan's house was still functional, tended by a last worshiper—Ibrihim Zlotny. He was thinner now, and no smile graced his furtive face. He scuttled from place to place carrying a laser rifle and barring each door behind him. And twice each day, he knelt before the stinking altar to ask in a whining voice for his reward. This was all a test, wasn't it? Or a joke? Surely the beautiful boats would come for him soon? Surely he would rise in the air and live forever?

But the forked-hooved figure in the hologram just leered and spoke not. Zlotny began to talk to himself and cast his blessings on followers who weren't there.

The poster blew onto the balcony and slid to Zlotny's feet. He paid it scant attention until the face in the picture caught his memory. Where had he seen that face? He picked up the poster and read it. Crick! Crick and Paterson! He read it again, eagerly. Then he turned and ran for the altar, his heart pounding. He threw himself on the floor. "Master, you have sent me a sign! I know now that you have more work for me before I receive your gift. I know what you want of me, and I am ready to do it. I live to serve you!"

He climbed to his feet, bowing awkwardly toward the altar, and hurried out of the room. In less than ten minutes, he was on the cracked road to Colorado Springs, bandoliers of laser batteries slung over his shoulders and his rifle held high.

He paused to rest two hours later. He was feverish and his eyes glittered. He realized that he was too weak to cross the country on foot.

Ahead of him, straddling the highway, stood the rusted hulk of a freightliner. Would it run? He made his way to it and climbed inside. He did not know how to start it, but fumbling with the switches eventually produced several lights on the dashboard. He pressed the accelerator experimentally. With a squeal of complaint, the Milk & Honey shuddered to life, shaking paint and rust flakes off her flanks in a fine cloud. Zlotny spun the wheel and aimed the lumbering giant east, into the rising sun.

* * * *

Grand Admiral Fegge-Gae sat on his crag in the center of the chamber. A sharp wind whistled around him, carrying selected odors designed to bring peace and judgment to his *krra*. On the ice below him, his concubines performed the poems of movement, their motions keyed to the shape of the chamber, the time, the number of Lorsii watching them, even the distance of the Great Boat above the planet of the hmmnns. Bloody light filled the chamber. It was as close an approximation of Joyworld as science, unlimited resource, and infinite patience could make it. It was a beautiful comment.

The admiral made the three-thousand-and-fourth royal form, *I am ready for business, although I would rather be making a poem.* He felt it was just the right compromise between the seriousness of the problem confronting them and the disdain a Lorsii should properly feel toward it.

A fleet captain sailed forward, her flight suggesting *ritual awe of high authority but determination to make a point.* "Thy eggs in poetry born, Admiral."

"And thine," he replied. "Thou say'st?"

She alit in beauty among his concubines. "Thy exquisiteness, I would trouble thee with a small curiosity."

"I am aware of the curiosity, Hokko-Lo. The beasts below have an amusing new weapon. The question is, what shall the Great People do about it?"

"Thy pardon. It is not a weapon the beasts have, for there is no technology the Great People have not mastered and we can detect not the means by which they thwart our toys."

"Wide is the universe, eggling-in-growth. Art certain the Great Folk know *all* sciences?"

"Doubtest thou this? Have we not made toys of races who moved suns about as an eggling's ball? Have we not entered the caves of illusion on flaming Arrkss and conquered? Have we not met the masters of time and played them like *veskkss* down the million-year war? What science can these humans have that answers no probe, registers on no instrument?"

The admiral sipped his wine from a goblet made from the skull of a being which had once ruled fifty suns. "Truth, though poor poetry."

Another fleet captain dropped off a crag and sailed down beside Hokko-Lo. From the bluntness of his motions and the agitation of his odor, the admiral knew him to be Kojja-Je. "Thy wingmate in beauty flying," he said, his wingtips forming *and so forth*. "The fact is, poetry or not, that the beasts have a power which we cannot fathom, and which has ceased to be amusing. I say we are for the Great Game here, and to oblivion with them."

There was a rustle of wings as the council formed *guarded agreement*.

The admiral postured *pronouncement of wisdom*. "The Great People have moved in beauty for ten million years. All we have found, we have conquered. All have been lesser forms, and all have ended. Does the fleet historian know how many peoples have fallen before the might of the Lorsii?"

The individual in question odored *intense interior search*. "Of the peoples of the inner suns, a hundred and nine millions. Of the peoples of the rims and arms, sixty millions. Of the peoples of the far darkness, all nine who have found us."

"And would'st thou know the count of *individuals* in those millions of peoples?"

She postured *regret with small beauty*. "As the suns themselves, Admiral. Beyond count."

"And of all the people of the universe, how many are left?"

There was silence, both of odor and posture, throughout the chamber. The admiral raised himself off his perch. "We have sailed three hundred years before finding this collection of beasts. Admiral Dukka-Da-Kre took her fleet to the edge of time and back and found nothing." He lifted into the air and circled lazily, his form and odor proclaiming *ultimate seriousness with overtones of sorrow*. "My captains, perhaps this is the last people. Perhaps the beasts below are all that is left." He landed beside a fountain of blood and wine trickling over ice. "Now, who speaks for the Great Game?"

After some moments, Kojja-Je fluttered and beat across the ice on his skatefeet. "This is a matter for all Joyworld, Admiral, and if true will be the greatest poem of all. But for now, let us deal with this Krrikk-beast. None in all the universe have defied the Great People and lived, and it should not happen now."

"Agreed, and please either control your emanations or kill yourself; you are disturbing my *krra*."

"Thy pardon, Admiral; thy pardons, sailors in this egg." The tall Lorsii made the form for *abject apology and attempt to restore beauty*.

Admiral Fegge-Gae made an odor of acceptance of apology and followed it with the thirty-fifth royal form, *decision boding amusement*. "Lest the beasts below cause cloudiness in our *krra*, let us take pleasure in their chastisement. Let us send a Great Boat upon them, that we may drink their agonies as we snuff them one by one.

A prize to the best poem to come from the killing! The royal wine to the best new form! The death of my eggling to the maker of the finest song!"

In a cloud of wings and chitterings, the Lorsii flapped into the air like so many locusts, entranced by the prospect of the coming entertainment. For the moment, their unease over the cause of the council was forgotten, and they turned their minds and *krras* from the thought that there might possibly be something in the universe stronger than themselves.

* * * *

Rebecca Martin wedged herself into a crotch between the trunk and a large limb and let her eye sweep the beautiful old hills. There were just enough deciduous trees mixed in the predominant pine and rhododendron to give a brush of color to the dark green mountainsides. The only time she had been through the Smoky Mountains before had been when she was a child, travelling with her father and mother in a 'steamer. In those days, she had assumed that the Smokies had their name from the eternal haze which was the gift of the Knoxville and Charlotte MillPlexes. But now, with both those cities reduced to shards and decay, she realized that the characteristic mist of the mountains was a product of heat and fine dew. She thought it incredibly lovely.

She had a moment's delicious fantasy, imagining that the thousands of campfire smoke columns rising in the still air belonged to the Cherokee and Tunica and Choctaw instead of her grandfather's followers; that it was half a thousand years ago— before the hunters in their buckskins, before the Pilgrims, before civilization. Before the Lorsii. Before the Lorsii.

The lovely fantasy dissolved, leaving the Smoky Mountains dark and brooding where they had been peaceful and inviting before.

Her mood changed, Rebecca scanned the valley a kilometer below. It had the look of a tribal gathering yet, for the encampment was mostly tents and lean-tos, interspersed with the occasional landcruiser and camper. Several long structures made of poles and roofed with canvas or pine needles or sod stood around the valley, providing hospitals and kitchens and even a sort of school: a mark of the faith the people showed in Josiah. Ever since the Bristol earthquake—"miracle," the people called it—that had swallowed up the howling mob of zombies who had come after them, the people were convinced that they were immune. And it seemed to be a well-founded belief, for the word had gotten around and the zombies were steering clear of their little valley.

The clear, high tolling of a bell rose from the valley and echoed around the hills. Rebecca's gaze went to the tiny church, a weathered relic, which the people had found when they came into the hills. It was without paint or pulpit, window glass or pews. But there was a roof and a bell and a baptismal font filled with zany frogs, and it had become the temple by instant and unanimous acclamation.

Now, as the little bell tolled, Rebecca saw Josiah come out of the building, all in white. At this distance he was just a dot, but she knew it was him: something about the way he moved or the way the other dots gathered toward him.

A wash of feelings went through her. Her love for the old man who was her grandfather was strong, but there was now another person in that bent old body, and her feelings for this new person were not so easily defined. She had the suspicion that this new person could see into her very soul.

"What troubles you, Rebecca?" he had asked the evening before.

She had bent over the cookfire, almost turning her back on him. "Nothing, Grandpa. Or do I have to call you Father Josiah, now?"

"Ahhh." He had come over and laid his hand in her hair, a gesture he had used since she had been about as high as his knee. "I am Josiah Crick, a sailor who plays a bad game of chess, remember? Sometimes known to my wilful granddaughter as 'Poppa-Bear.'"

"Poppa-Bear didn't perform miracles. Neither did Josiah Crick."

He sat himself on the log which served them for both chair and table, and leaned on his staff. "Neither does Father Josiah, Becky. Only God performs miracles."

She poured beans and corn into a bowl and brought him a spoon. "Grandpa, you scare me, now. When you get up and point that stick of yours, something weird always happens. It's like—like you're not *human* anymore!"

Crick ignored his food, watching the woman through his spectacles. "I know what you mean, child. I always feel frightened afterwards—as though the Lord had taken me over right down to the hair in my beard, and that's a powerful and fearsome thing. Sometimes, afterward, I feel like I'm going to throw up." He mused, pulling at his beard. "I wonder if Isaiah or Jeremiah felt like that?"

"That's another thing, Poppa-Bear. I can't help feeling that it's blasphemous for you to think of yourself as a prophet. That was two or three thousand years ago, Grandpa, in Bible times."

"There were probably a thousand years between some of the early prophets and some of the later ones, child. And it's still Bible times; it always is and always will be." He had noticed his food and took a bite or two. "As to its being blasphemous, my actin' the prophet, who's to say that all the prophets have been used up? Maybe God's got a hundred more saved up for the next million years or so? An' remember that no one was born a prophet. Even the disciples were men of the world before God laid His hand on them."

"So you *do* believe you're one?"

"I believe God's found a use for me aside from trying to bring up a Christian young woman, an' that He's using me now. I've felt that since I first knew of Ibrihim Zlotny."

She had stirred her food moodily, avoiding his eyes. "It still scares me, all these miracles you do."

"God does, Becky. I'm just something He's using to call attention to them." He had leaned across the log and taken both her hands in his. "What's really scaring you, child, is the fact you can't get around: that it *is* God, and these *are* miracles. You're troubled in your soul because you just can't make yourself believe in what you're seeing. You don't want your faith to jump out of the Bible and be an everyday thing. You want it to be history, not current events." The look in her eyes told him he was right. "Well, Becky, don't be too hard on yourself. God never gives His faithful a load they can't carry. If this is Armageddon and the end is at hand, I have no doubt that you will be firm in your belief, and that God will take you to His bosom."

And now, sitting in the tree above the valley, she thought of the words she had wanted to say the night before, but hadn't: Yes, but I don't want it to be now. I want to live!

There was a rustle in the underbrush behind her, and she scrambled down the tree to grab her pistol. "Password, or I'll blow your brains out."

A young man pushed his way out of the undergrowth, his face fearful. "Second Timothy, two/five. They're coming!"

"Who's coming?"

"The bugs! Oh, Lord, the Lorsii are coming!"

* * * *

CHAPTER FIFTEEN

Jon Paterson felt the electric tingle of the nutrient web withdrawing. It coagulated and sucked itself back into the orifices from which it had issued, leaving Paterson naked on the cold floor of the chamber. What was it this time, he wondered with hatred. Another performance for the folks back home? Another probing of the vile machines? Or was he to be left alone to wander the vessel again—a process which appeared to amuse his captors. Whatever it was, though, this time it would be different. This time, he swore silently, he was going to escape. He knew a little, now, about controlling his odor, about masking his emotions. He knew enough to fake them off for a few minutes. He hoped.

A short Lorsii whose clipped wings and face jewels marked him as ego-indentured waved Paterson out of the chamber. "Come, hmmnn. Hass-Ka-Ve wish speak you."

Paterson got off the floor and nodded. "Right, monster. Nothing like a friendly little chat with the neighborhood butchers." He stepped around the Lorsii and militantly strode off toward Hass-Ka-Ve's chambers, knowing that he was revealing how much he'd learned about the layout of the boat but needing to take some sort of defiant attitude. Let the damned bug follow *him*.

Hass-Ka-Ve sat folded into the ninth form for meditation, *preparation for discussion*. Paterson noted that her handmaidens' postures were slightly scandalized and correctly assumed that it was because he was the object of the preparation. Lorsii did not discuss anything with 'lower forms.' They only killed them.

Paterson planted his feet and stood before Hass-Ka-Ve in surly defiance. "Okay, bug. Talk."

She made an infinitely grave motion and indicated that he sit. "Wish discuss this."

Paterson saw that she held a Bible. He grimaced and squatted on the floor. "Somehow that book looks soiled in your hand."

"Why? Because you hate Lorsii? Say here Jesus take book among sinners, yes? That not purpose of book?"

He glowered but had to nod agreement. "Yeah. But the Word goes to those who want to hear it, not to those who mock it. Any sinner is welcome in a church, but churches are cleaned and reconsecrated after they've been defiled by those who come to mock and laugh."

"I am not laugh, Jnn-Pttrsan."

Paterson studied her closely. Her posture, as sketchily as he could read it, was of utmost sincerity. He nodded again. "Okay, so you're not laughing. So what? Now you know the difference between good and evil. Are you going to stop the slaughter of my people?"

"No. Not sure yet this song valid. Interesting, yes. New philosophy. Add greatly to *krra* of race. Curious thought. Besides, can't change whole *krra* of race alone."

"Jesus did."

"You think my song strong as Jesus?"

"Don't blaspheme, monster."

Hass-Ka-Ve sat serene, studying the Bible in her hand. "Very difficult learn read your language, your book. Concepts not coherent." She tapped the Bible with a clawed finger. "Teach here wrong to hurt, wrong to lie, wrong to use other hmmnn. But same people make joke over other hmmnn misfortune. Routine-all-time practice lie, cheat, steal, call it 'business.' Routine-all-time oppress, kill, torture in name of Lord. Where different from Lorsii?"

Paterson rocked on his haunches, drawn in in spite of himself. "That's an old question, Hass-Ka-Ve. And I'm not the one to answer it. I'm not a preacher, I'm a scientist. I guess it's just that we're all faced every day with the choice of being good or evil. Most of us don't make the right choice very often."

She nodded in a conscious effort to make the human gesture of agreement. "Much like Lorsii. Right choice lift *krra* of race, wrong one lower *krra*. Difference that you think right and wrong one thing, we think another."

"We don't enjoy killing."

"Yes, you do. Many, many book show this."

"Okay, okay. But we think the people who *do* enjoy it are evil."

She closed the Bible and held it on her thorax. "You think me monster, yes?"

"Yes. Well—" Paterson felt confused.

"Say here in Bible *all* beings belong God. All beings His children, yes?"

"I guess so. I mean, yes, it does say that."

"Then you, me, both God's creatures, brother, sister, yes?"

It was too much. Paterson leapt up, his face red. "Brother and sister! Listen, you swine, after what you've done to me and my people, you could only be a sister to the devil. Those obscene 'love' scenes! The casual killing, the burning, the—the filth!" Rage made him inarticulate.

Hass-Ka-Ve moved a wingtip. Her handmaidens came up. She chittered in her own language. "The hmmnn is upset. Please take him back to the nourishment web. I shall cleanse the chamber of his rage."

Paterson caught bits of it and started to make caustic comment. Then he stopped himself. Only one of the handmaidens was coming toward him. Perhaps this would be the chance he was looking for. He allowed himself to be escorted out of the chamber.

Hass-Ka-Ve sat in a posture of intense thought, pleased on two points. She had managed to provoke the human into revealing the depth of his early conditioning: even a scientist, if pushed hard enough, retained a respect for and a belief in this Jesus. And a point which caused an odd flutter in her hearts: Paterson had, though he didn't seem aware of it, referred to her by name. For that small moment, he had treated her as another rational being. And though he was a lower form, a beast, a being with a song the color of mud, the beautiful Lorsii could not help feeling somehow flattered and proud that she had achieved this status with him.

* * * *

At a curve in the corridor leading to the nourishment web, Paterson slowed and stopped. He raised his foot to peer at the sole as if he had stepped on something sharp. The Lorsii handmaiden stopped and bent curiously to peer with him, a reflex gesture. Her triangular head was less than a foot above Paterson's own. With a quick prayer for success and forgiveness, he whipped a hard uppercut at what would have been the point of a human's jaw. His whole arm went numb as his fist struck the chitinous exoskeleton, but the Lorsii folded in half and went to the floor with a complete lack of grace. Try *that* form on for size, Paterson thought with hard satisfaction as he loped down the corridor.

It took him some time to find his way from the part of the boat where he'd been held to the part which contained the swanboats and the landing platform. The Great Boats were, like everything else Lorsii he'd seen, a fantasyland illusion of hidden mechanisms, concealed lightbeams and odd passages. It was the Lorsii way to make everything subservient, and they did so with their machinery, hiding it away as if to avoid reminding themselves that they were, in the end, dependent on hydraulics and electricity rather than their vaunted *krra*.

Ducking and dodging, moving awkwardly through passages meant for winged beings, Paterson came at last to the bitter cold open passageway that led to the landing platform. He stole across a floor made of the frozen, polished corpses of some octopoid race, their lavender eyes still staring in mute horror. The door to the landing platform was directly before him. He could see a swanboat through it, outlined against the sky. And in the doorway, its back to him, a Lorsii sat in a pose of contemplation. This one was something about mathematics, one of their comments on the unity of things, which was a comment on harmony and harmonics. All that interested Paterson about this knowledge was that it implied oblivion of his presence. He crept forward, his fists balled.

Without moving, the Lorsii spoke. "To drink the wine, hmmnn."

"To feel the wind," Paterson responded, speaking before he realized it. He leapt back, blinking, his fists held in front of him.

The Lorsii unfolded itself, shaking out its beautiful wings. "You wish kill me? Will you make beautiful comment? Drink my death?" It advanced on Paterson, not hostile, but as if in invitation. "Not hard kill Lorsii."

"Yeah, bug, I know. I just clipped one of your flunkies. You want to be next, just step up. No need to take a number."

The Lorsii stopped, his hands held wide and obviously empty. "Name you Jnn-Pttrsan. Name me Kojja-Je. Wingmate Hass-Ka-Ve."

Paterson blinked again, lowering his guard ever so slightly. "Oh, yeah. I know you now. You're the bug she sent over the side when she tricked me into falling."

Kojja-Je indicated agreement. "You wish leave ship. I wish you leave. I help you."

Paterson frowned. "Why would a bug want to help me do anything besides die for his amusement?"

"Hass-Ka-Ve my wingmate." Even in the awkwardness of an alien tongue, his anguish came through.

Paterson lowered his hands to his side. "Well, I'll be—" The idea

that this stinking insect was jealous—and of *him*—was too ludicrous for Paterson's comprehension. Yet, the form and odor Kojja-Je displayed were too blatant and too sincere to be trickery. For the merest flicker of a second, Paterson felt both pity and a kind of comradeship for the winged being.

But it passed. "Okay, buddy. My heart bleeds for you, but what I want now is off the trolly. If you want to help, that's fine. Any tricks, though, and I'll brain you."

Kojja-Je looked around, then picked up a slim tool and handed it to Paterson. "Point. Press here. Think poem. It send beam of light and kill." He stood directly in front of the weaponlike tool. "Come. We go boat, go down. I leave you there."

* * * *

Charlotte Honesdale lowered her shovel wearily, watching President Falstrom pat the last lumps of dirt onto the grave.

"It's ironic," Falstrom said, puffing a little. "Charlie went through three wars, was bombed out of two embassies, and survived an assassination attempt. It's ridiculous to live that adventurous a life only to be killed by snakebite."

"The snake was incidental, Lars. The ambassador was sixty-three years old, and we've been doing thirty kilos a day for the past week. He was worn out."

"Aren't we all." Falstrom tossed his own shovel aside and sagged against the shed beside which they had dug the grave. "Well, at least Charlie made it to America. He always wanted to be assigned here and never got it."

Charlotte looked toward the three people with them, who waited beside the old Dodge several meters away. Five people; all that was left of the government of the planet Earth. She wondered in passing if the three—a file clerk and two couriers—should be raised to cabinet rank.

"Do you know this area?" Falstrom asked.

"Vaguely. Charlestown is over that way. If we stay on this highway, we should get into the mountains in three days."

"I hope that's time enough."

The last report that had come into the bunker before the zombies had flooded them out had told of a leisurely but continual movement of the Lorsii Great Boats, all on courses whose plots intersected in the Great Smoky Mountains of America: in a long, narrow valley filled with Christians. Even at the waltz-time pace of their coming, the arrival of the Lorsii was a matter of days and possibly of hours.

"I hope it's worth the effort," the American Secretary said. In two locked briefcases and a steel strongbox, they carried that last analysis the government had been able to make on the invaders, the last data that had been collected. Charlotte Honesdale could not help thinking what a small—and perhaps futile—collection it was, in light of all the people who had suffered and died to collect it. Even if the conclusions it contained proved right, what use would they be? How could the knowledge be turned into a weapon sufficient to check the horrible power of the Lorsii?

President Falstrom groaned and picked up his shovel. "We'd best get moving. I don't like to be out in the open this much. That last bunch of zombies nearly got us."

Charlotte accepted the hand he held out and let him pull her to her feet. "It's not them I'm worried about, Lars."

"What do you mean?"

"Well, an awful lot of people are heading toward Father Josiah right now, and a lot of them are zombies. If I were the Christians, and were getting ready to fight off the Lorsii, I'd be suspicious of newcomers." She slung her shovel over her shoulder and headed for the Dodge. "In fact, if it were me, I'd shoot first and ask questions later."

* * * *

Beelzebub stuck his snout around the corner of the wall, his little eyes like glass beads and his whiskers twitching. The cat was several meters across the floor, Crick marginally closer. The mouse decided to chance it and took off.

Hezekiah lifted one eyelid, his slit-pupiled eye tracking the mouse. At just the right moment, he pounced, leaping along a tail's length behind the scurrying rodent.

Beelzebub scuttled up Josiah's robe with a squeak of terror and dove into the old man's beard just as Hezekiah leapt on Crick's stomach. Josiah sat up with a *whuff* of surprise, his glasses sliding down his nose. "Here, now, what's this?"

Hezekiah curled into a contented ball on his lap, and the mouse peeked out of his whiskers. "Well, bless me! Now I'm a racetrack, am I?" He tickled both animals fondly.

The door swung open and Rebecca Martin strode into the church.

"Now, Becky, I've told you not to bring weapons into the House of the Lord."

She came up to the rocking chair in which he sat, her fists clinched and tears in her eyes. "They're leaving, Poppa-Bear. They're running out on us."

"Who, child?"

"All those good Christians out there. Hundreds and hundreds of them. They're sneaking off into the hills in hopes the Lorsii won't spot them. We've got more going out than coming in—and the ones who are leaving are taking food and weapons with them. Most everybody coming in is barehanded and starving."

"Now, calm down, Rebecca. The faint of heart and poor of faith always run away. They are no less loved by God for that."

"Grandpa, it's not *fair*. We took them in and fed them and doctored them, and now that it's time to stand up and fight, they're deserting us."

Josiah put the cat on the floor and got up. "Well, perhaps those coming in will be made of sterner stuff."

She snorted. "At least one out of five is a zombie trying to get at you, or somebody on the edge of collapse. What with guarding the zombie prisoners and tending the sick and lame, half of the fighting force we've got left is tied up."

Josiah picked up his ever-present Bible and his staff. "It doesn't matter anyway, Rebecca. Weapons aren't going to win this battle. Nothing but faith and the grace of God will sustain us. I have let the people arm themselves and fortify our encampment because that is what they know; that is the way battles have always been prepared for. But when the moment comes, their prayers and not their guns will save them." He tapped her rifle with his staff. "Will that bring down a Lorsii ship? Will a lasercannon blast one single Lorsii from the sky?"

She sighed. "I doubt it. But what else can we do?"

"What we've done since the time of Eden: pray."

There was a commotion outside. Rebecca and the patriarch looked toward the door. Two children burst in, their faces red with excitement. "Come quick," one cried. "They've caught the Great Servant!"

Rebecca threw her grandfather a look of triumph and hatred. "Zlotny! You get your wish after all, Grandpa." Then she ran for the door.

Josiah raised a hand after her, but saw he was too late. "Gently, child," he called, knowing she would not hear him. "Gently."

Rebecca ran down the valley, collecting people as she went. They followed her excitement at first, then, as the news of its cause reached them, they followed their own revenge. Guns and knives flashed in the light, sticks and fist-sized rocks were waved in the air. Seven or eight hundred strong, they streamed past the circled emplacements of campers, cars, and freightliner tractors, the zigzagged trenches, the sharpened-stake fencerows, all pointing toward the narrow entrance to the valley and the hasty earthen rampart which blocked it.

Through the one small gate in the rampart, a large group of Christians came running, led by a man on a horse. He had a rope tied to his saddle, and the other was tied around the wrists of a man being dragged across the stony ground. Those running along beside him were throwing rocks and sticks at him.

"Stop it," Rebecca yelled in the loudest voice she could muster. "He belongs to Father Josiah!"

The name quelled the mob a little. The horseman slowed his mount to a trot, then a walk.

Rebecca stationed herself in front of the people who had followed her down the valley, and her finger was on the trigger of her rifle. She was not all that sure she could control her own hatred long enough to deliver Zlotny to her grandfather.

The horseman dragged his burden up to Rebecca and dismounted, a bit ashamed of himself but with hatred still on his face. "Here he is, Sister. Let Father Josiah have him, then. But let us watch!"

Rebecca walked over to the dirt- and blood-crusted figure lying face down in the dirt, and she felt light in the head. Almost of its own volition, the rifle swung in her hands. Her teeth were gritted and her face contorted with the struggle. "Look at me," she said, her voice thick and slurred. "Look me in the face."

The man raised his head, wobbly and glazed-eyed. "Hello, Rebecca," he said through bloody teeth. "Take me to the captain."

It was Jon Paterson.

* * * *

CHAPTER SIXTEEN

Grand Admiral Fegge-Gae lay on a plle board, having his wing jewels polished by his concubines. He did not bother looking around when Kojja-Je sailed into the chamber and came skating across the floor. "Greetings, favored eggmate." His position, tone, and odor indicated that Kojja-Je was anything but favored at the moment.

Kojja-Je made a totally graceless bow. "Thy song ever onward, My Master."

The Grand Admiral waved his concubines to one side and sat up, preening. "I have often wondered how you rose to a position of prominence, Admiral—considering that you have no control over your emotions and less over your actions. Please see to your dignity; you are sullying this chamber." He waited while the waves of fear and apology and defiance became a more-or-less smooth harmonic on the wind, then faced his subordinate. "Well, now. I learn that you have taken it upon yourself to free the beast whom Hass-Ka-Ve was keeping as a pet. This is so?"

"It is so, My Admiral. But—"

"And you were aware when so doing that I had arranged for this beast's being here? That it was for my amusement that it had been brought here? That I personally had chosen to use this beast to chastise the Zlltnnee beast?"

"I was aware, Grand Admiral."

"And still you did this thing?" Fegge-Gae felt a stirring of curiosity; his calculated attack was not having quite the expected effect on Kojja-Je. There was an urgency in the lower admiral's posture, and perhaps a sense of power, as if Kojja-Je were holding something important to use in a final gamble.

Kojja-Je made the posture of agreement. "I did, My Admiral."

"So. And perhaps you would care to tell me why?"

"I would, Master of my nest. I released the Pttrsan because he was dangerously sullying the *krra* of this ship, of the people aboard it, and especially of my wingmate, Hass-Ka-Ve."

The Grand Admiral stood, shaking out his wings in a deliberately casual fashion. "That is a powerful word, 'dangerously.' It implies that this beast had the power to impinge on a Lorsii. Or perhaps merely on a *weak* Lorsii, mmm?"

Kojja-Je stood unmoving, avoiding the insult. "The Pttrsan interested my wingmate in a book of the beasts."

"Book?"

"A primitive recording device. This one is called 'Bible' and holds a version of the beasts' *krra*."

"Like the song-tubes of the NumumUmmna?"

"Like but unlike, apparently. At least, Hass-Ka-Ve thinks thus. She has troubled to learn the language of the beasts, and has read this Bible of theirs." His posture held a dangerous defiance. "And Hass-Ka-Ve, My Admiral, is not a weak Lorsii."

The Grand Admiral studied Kojja-Je closely. "No, she isn't. And this book has—influenced her?"

"I believe, so. Adversely."

"On what do you base this belief?"

"On the fact that she questions the supremacy of the Great People. On the fact that her own *krra* has grown cloudy. On the fact that she has—has—"

"Ahhh. There is an attraction to the beast, then?"

"It's ridiculous, Sire! It's monstrous! And it is true."

Fegge-Gae made the form for slightly risque humor. "I thought it was anatomically impossible?" He registered a small triumph at twisting the words into Kojja-Je's wound. He wrapped himself in his wings and began leisurely skating around the chamber, apparently intent only on demonstrating his skill at several difficult forms. "So at heart what we have here is a case of jealousy. Considering the object of your feelings, and the fact of its being a beast, the situation has its ludicrous aspects. But I can find no basis for danger here. And thus, Admiral-of-the-uncontrolled-emotions, no basis for forgiving your action." He skated to a sharp stop directly in front of Kojja-Je, his posture one of threatened violence. "You have displeased me."

Kojja-Je stood his ground, his wingtips flared in a posture of pugnaciousness. "Perhaps the Grand Admiral has not considered all aspects of the problem as yet." His odor connoted that Fegge-Gae's failure to do so implied stupidity.

The Grand Admiral calmed instantly. Kojja-Je's insult was almost deadly. "I grant you there is danger in this chamber, Kojja-Je." He folded himself into a cone of alert stillness, like a coiled snake. "Beware of whom that danger seeks."

"Danger seeks all, My Leader. The Great People have ever sought danger. I did not become an admiral by avoiding danger."

Fegge-Gae relaxed. "Thy bravery is known to all Joyworld, Admiral Kojja-Je-cragrider. And proven here. Few would stand so boldly before my anger. I listen with all humility to your assessment of the danger we face. Speak, then. There is nothing at stake but your life."

It worked. Kojja-Je defused. He spoke in the rapid chitter of his kind, detailing what Hass-Ka-Ve had told him of the contents of the Bible. He reiterated the ongoing oddities encountered by the Zlotnyites when confronting Crick and his bristly band. And he spoke of Paterson's accomplishment in gathering knowledge of the Great Boat and the Lorsii language despite his drugging. At last he was finished, though his odor and the position of his legs relative to the Admiral made it clear that not all was said.

Fegge-Gae arched off the ice and flew a time, deep in contemplation. When he landed near Kojja-Je, his posture told the graceless admiral that he was convinced. "You shall live, my eggmate, and have my thanks in the bargain. But I am not so sure of Hass-Ka-Ve. She is a dreamer, that one, a poet and a singer. If her *krra* has become warped, she cannot be allowed to spread the poison." He turned to observe the reaction to his statement. "I'm sorry. She will have to be confined."

Kojja-Je odored a stange mixture of fear, joy and triumph. "I'm afraid that cannot be arranged, My Leader."

"You defy me?"

"Time does. Even now, Hass-Ka-Ve enters the Null-Chambers. She will emerge a Srra, or near."

* * * *

CHAPTER SEVENTEEN

Hass-Ka-Ve drifted through the nautiloid chambers of the Great Boat's *krra*-clearing section, her wings undulating idly like becalmed sails. The essence of the chambers was total nullification of external forces, so completely maintained that not only the gravity of the planet below, but its Coriolis effect was blanked out. No breath of wind moved in the chambers. The temperature of the air was at Lorsii neutral—in human terms, about two degrees Celsius. The light was, if anything, beige.

Hass-Ka-Ve drifted past galaxies made of jewels spinning in voids of velvet-moss; tiny suns made of fluorescent gems from the inner ears of an exterminated race, circled by pinprick rubies and emeralds, diamonds and sapphires, all pavaned on an erratic ellipsis dictated by the mood of the fluorescent gems.

She drifted, her motion supplied, as was intended, by the minuscule currents of air flowing into and out of her spiracles, her life itself the force which directed her progress toward the innermost chamber: a comment on eternity.

Her form was formlessness, the null-form, *I exist only within my krra. I am free of externals.*

She was here in the chambers in search of the guiding poem, for she was faced with decisions which would alter her *krra*, and thus her portion of the race's, forever. Whatever she decided, her existence would take a new direction, and the waves beating out from her change of course would wash against every Lorsii alive and yet to live.

Her time in the chambers was timelessness, and she was not aware of its passage. But when she made her decisions and came again into the second reality—the life through the senses—she was dehydrated and ravenous. She was dimly aware, through her still-introspective state, that she had reached the innermost-but-one chamber, a comment which would add jewels to her wings for the rest of her life. Though none were there to verify it, she knew she would be believed implicitly, for she bore in the plates of her thighs the opals and garnets of the sixth form for personal bondage, *never to lie.*

She made her way out of the chambers, her motions those of exhaustion and her passage sullying the purity of the place. It would take weeks to restore the chambers to neutrality, and this was a comment.

Outside, wine and burnt flesh awaited, placed there by the attendants of the chambers, and Hass-Ka-Ve disciplined herself to partake of them slowly, with grace and proper disdain. Her eighty-fourth form, *taking sustenance as ritual,* was shaky, but she knew this would reflect favorably, a comment on the intensity of her time in the chambers. With a small, fierce pride, she knew the certainty of there being a poem or at least a song to come from this. Already one of the chamber attendants had postured himself into *creative effort to honor another.*

Another attendant skated up deferentially. "Thou, through the flames."

"And thou, in halos shining."

"To the innermost chamber, Hass-Ka-Ve-Srra?"

"But one; I rate not the kindness of the title yet."

"But one! Thy *krra* is a sun to light our way. Thou hast honored this ship and all the Great Folk unto the death of the universe."

"Thy kindness, eggmate. Thy kindness."

Lorsii were gathering as the news spread. While she ate and drank, the room filled with quiet, admiring voyagers. An odor chant went up, wafted through the room on precise, syncopated flutters of a hundred wingtips. Here and there, an acrid whiff of the tenth form for adoration came on the breeze: an odor normally reserved for royalty or a noble death.

The Grand Admiral skated into the room and made a gracious bow of arms and wings. "Thou, bringer of honor to my ship."

"And thou, keeper of my *krra.*"

"Would'st consent to speak to me on my perch, that I may know thy revelations?"

"Thy command is my joy." She rose and followed him out, borne as much by the chant of the gathered Lorsii as by her feeble wingbeats.

They came into the admiral's quarters and alit on his crag. Even as they landed, he indicated that his concubines and attendants leave, and in a short time they were alone.

"Wine?"

"No. I am nourished."

The admiral laid himself along a perch made from a single, enormous ruby two meters long and a meter thick. "I am sensitive, Hass-Ka-Ve, to the curious attention you have paid to the Jnn-Pttrsan, and your clouded *krra* since it left us."

"It is a matter of no concern, Admiral. I fret for a lost amusement."

"That is perilously close to a lie."

She made the form for *wry acknowledgment*. "It is but part of the truth. Still, it is a personal concern."

"Everything is the concern of a fleet admiral, especially the personal matters of one who has been within one chamber of acquiring the title of Srra." His posture and odor were relaxed, but his aura brooked no evasion. It was not for nothing that he wore the emeralds of power in his wings.

Hass-Ka-Ve postured *submission to superior* krra, knowing that the admiral would read it as both an admission and a reminder of her own new-won power. "The Jnn-Pttrsan is a beast of power, My Admiral. It is as though he were in some *krra*-clearing chamber of his own, and nearing the innermost chamber. I cannot help feeling that he will have an effect on the Great Folk."

"'He'? Would'st give the beast equality with the Lorsii?"

"Equality? No, My Admiral. Perhaps something greater."

The fleet commander's shock was displayed in all his aspects. "Thou sailest strange skies, even for a near-Srra."

"I speak as my *krra* directs me."

Fegge-Gae toyed with a bowl of acid candy. "And does your *krra* give you words concerning how the Jnn-Pttrsan shall affect the Great Folk?"

She was thoughtful, quiet for so long that the admiral thought she had retreated into her *krra*. "No," she said at last, "but it will be revealed when the fleet comes upon him and his followers tomorrow."

"You mean, 'the Krrikk's followers,' don't you?"

"Ah, yes, of course."

* * * *

The courier came out of the trees with his hands high and holding a white rag tied on a stick. As he approached the rampart, a white-robed man with a pistol stood up behind it. "Stop there, stranger."

The courier stopped.

"State your business."

"I'm with the government. President Falstrom and Secretary Honesdale are back there. They're hurt. We want in."

"There's no government anymore. Not here, not anywhere."

"I know. We're it. We've come from The Hague."

"The valley's closed."

"We've got information for Josiah Crick."

"Father Josiah is praying. You'd best do the same." The man considered a moment. "Bring the President and the Secretary out here where we can see them."

The courier turned and motioned. Falstrom came out of the trees, dragging a travois with the strongbox and briefcases on it. Charlotte Honesdale followed him, walking backwards and swinging her rifle in an arc to cover the trees behind. They came up to the rampart and stood beside the courier.

Other heads appeared over the ramparts. There was a whispered conference. The gate swung open. "Leave your weapons on the ground; we'll bring them in for you. Enter one at a time. Keep your hands up."

They did as they were told and were shuffled through the gate. Each was questioned by determined-looking people, probed, cross-examined, searched for weapons, and finally turned over to Rebecca Martin, who looked haggard and overworked. "Peace be with you," she said. "For the moment at least."

Falstrom, in obvious pain from a wound in his side, indicated the precious strongbox and briefcases. "I'd like to get these to Father Josiah. They contain our findings on the Lorsii and might be of some use to him."

"Poppa-Bear can use any help he can get right about now," she said, then laughed at the look on their faces. "Josiah's my grandfather. Come on, I'll see if he's busy. Then we'll look to your hurts."

They walked up the valley, stepping aside for marching columns of armed Christians and wagons loaded with weaponry. "I'm impressed," Honesdale said, "with your efficiency. I can understand now how you've managed to stave off the zombies."

"Wrong," Rebecca replied. "There's been almost no actual fighting. It's all been Grandpa's work—and the Lord's."

President Falstrom smiled. "Yes, I've heard about the miracles.

We've got an explanation for them here in our reports. It's part of what we've learned about the Lorsii."

"Oh?" Rebecca's tone was casual, but it didn't fool Charlotte Honesdale, who tried to shush the president.

He did not see her motion, and plunged ahead. "You, see, it all ties in with this *krra* concept of theirs, a kind of psionic projection they do. It affects everything around them, so that when something throws it out of focus, it upsets the electrical balance of the environment. That's what caused the earthquakes and the lightning strikes. That's—"

"That's wrong," Rebecca said with conviction. "God caused those things."

Falstrom stopped speaking, hearing the tone in her voice. "Yes, perhaps so." With diplomatic skill, he changed the subject. "You seem to be well organized here. What's in that tent over there?"

"A chapel, a nursery, and forty-six cases of hand grenades."

"Mmm. And that one, the one which is so heavily guarded?"

"Jon Paterson."

* * * *

The old man peered into the still depths of the pool, marveling for a moment at its clarity. Tiny fish swam lazily in its lower reaches, seeming to float on air, so crystalline were the waters. Then he pulled his attention back to the pool's surface and his own image, reflected in it. He wished for as much clarity there as in the waters. Was the man looking back at him Elmer Crick the sailor, or Father Josiah the patriarch and tool of God? Or perhaps just an old fool with delusions?

But he knew, deep in his heart, that however he saw himself, he was doing what was expected of him, and that was all that counted. If only he knew what was expected of him in this coming trial!

He felt a moment's guilt at his worry. God had always spoken when the time was right.

"Father Josiah."

He looked around. "Yes, my son?"

"I'm sorry to disturb you, but Sister Rebecca says you should come back down in the valley. It's too hard to guard you up here."

"I have a Guardian, son, and He is always with me."

The boy looked doubtfully at Hezekiah, then blushed as he realized who Josiah was talking about. "Er, Sister Rebecca also says that Paterson is awake now and asking for you." The boy's face was grim. "I don't think you should talk to him, Father. He's evil. He'll contaminate you!"

Josiah picked up the cat. "He is God's servant, just as we all are. Only lack of faith can contaminate anyone."

"Yes, Father."

The patriarch stepped out of the glade, looking skyward. Overhead, to the south, Zlotny's horned cross was dying. The pieces had flown so far apart now that only by searching them out could you separate them from the sun-glare. Several of the pieces had flamed out and were no longer visible at all. In God's grace, Josiah thought, they had returned to their original innocence, now merely dead rocks coursing through the airlessness. "All right, son. Let's go see Jon Paterson."

As they came down the mountain, people smiled at Josiah, many kneeling or making the sign of the cross as he passed. Some called out to him, either in defiant shouts to show their willingness in the forthcoming fight or in humble need for his own strength to augment theirs. All of them knew, as did Josiah himself, that a million zombies were closing in on their valley in a ring of death and hatred, and that the Great Boats of the Lorsii floated above them. And each of them knew that their enemies were less than twenty-four hours away. Zealots of the Army of the Final Testament were already picking their way over the ridges to hurl threats and bullets and laserbeams at the outer ring of defenses. To the north and east, the mountains themselves were being burned.

At the guarded tent, Father Josiah tried to chase off the men and women who surrounded it, but they would not go. All he could do was keep them outside.

Paterson was sitting up in his bed as Josiah entered. Rebecca Martin sat on a chair nearby, her rifle across her knees and her fingers on the trigger. Paterson smiled wanly. "So, Captain Crick. Every time we meet, I'm either at death's door or under guard—or both."

Josiah smiled warmly and sat on the end of the bed. "We're all at death's door every moment of our lives, Jon. And we're all under guard. God's guard. How do you feel?"

"How do I look?"

"Ten years older, sick, and jubilant."

Paterson's grin was half humor, half acknowledgment. "That's exactly how I feel." His grin faded in a hoarse cough that went on and on, shaking him and the bed. He fumbled for a napkin, and Rebecca reluctantly handed him one. He thanked her with his eyes as he coughed up blood, but she made a point of ignoring his thanks.

When he could speak, he turned a serious face to Josiah. "Captain Crick, we're going to beat the Lorsii. In fact, you're going to do it."

"God will decide that, Jon."

Paterson made an impatient motion with his hand. "Whatever. Look, I understand them now."

Rebecca snorted. "I'll just bet you do."

Paterson went on as though she'd not spoken. "I know what makes them tick, Captain. They're missing something; they've got a loose screw, and that's where we're going to get them."

Josiah nodded, smiling as though he were a step ahead of the gaunt man on the bed.

"It's weird, you know. They've been around for half a billion years. They've thought of everything, tried everything, worn everything out. And in all that time, they never stumbled on the one thing that separates us from them—us from every creature we know about." He leaned across the bed and took Josiah's hand in his. "Captain, they have no concept of right and wrong. They have no morality!"

Josiah beamed as though Paterson were a student who had just solved a difficult problem. "Of course not, Jon. They've not known God."

"But they will! I've *seen* it." Paterson went off in his wracking cough again and waved Rebecca back. "My dreams, my 'nightmares,' you remember the original one?"

"I think so."

"Remember what I was seeing? An old man with a grey beard, facing the Lorsii on the ice. And he was preaching the Gospel to them! That's how it's going to happen, Captain. They're going to take you back to Joyworld, and you're going to teach them right from wrong!"

Josiah's face was sad, gentle, but he continued to nod and smile.

Rebecca Martin stepped up, glowering. "That's baloney. How do you think your visions will turn into reality?"

"They weren't visions. The Lorsii have some kind of control over them, in little ways. It has to do with their *krra*."

Rebecca twitched, hearing Jon Paterson use the exact phrase President Falstrom had used. For an instant, she wondered if both of the men were right.

"Every now and then," Paterson continued, not noticing the woman's movement, "they lose a piece of the energy they use to control things—a kind of bleed-over effect. That's what happened to me, why I was getting bits and pieces of the *krra* they were pouring into Zlotny and his creeps. And some of that *krra* as previews of the future." He turned to the woman and spoke parenthetically. "That's how they get through space. They do a—a form that includes seeing themselves where they want to be, and *whap!*—there they are."

149

The woman chewed her lip. "There's a couple of parts I don't like about this, Jon. If I remember your vision correctly, it had the earth being destroyed."

Paterson laid back against his pillow, spent. "Yes, that's the way I saw it." He turned troubled eyes on Josiah Crick.

The patriarch smiled. "I remember, too, Jon. The man who carried the Word to the Lorsii in your vision died there on the ice, didn't he?"

* * * *

CHAPTER EIGHTEEN

Admiral Fegge-Gae odored *pleasant diversions with overtones of revenge* as he leaned over the Great Boat's bowsprit. Below, the mountains were aflame. The land crawled from horizon to horizon with Zlotnyites converging on the little valley just ahead.

Above and behind him, spread in a fan, were the hundred Great Boats of his fleet; swanboats and airborne Lorsii drifted languidly among and between them. It was a grand and glorious sight, and Fegge-Gae was hard put not to let his posture show that it bored him. How many hundreds of times had this scene been repeated? And with how many more worthy adversaries? He could remember races who took a Great Boat with them as they died, races who went to their ends in fine, howling hatred, races who obliterated themselves rather than give the Lorsii the satisfaction of doing it.

But these hmmnns...they squatted in their little valley for all the world as though the Lorsii weren't there. Their fellow beasts flung fire and ruin at them, and they did not respond.

Not entirely true, the admiral corrected himself. They sang. But there was no power in the song, no force, no *krra*.

Still, it was a disquieting, Lorsii-like response, and Fegge-Gae had an instant of what could only be fear, wondering if the song of the hmmnns might hold a power he simply could not see.

He put the thought from him at once and turned to his helmsman. "Stop the boat. Let us take wine and watch the beasts fling themselves at one another."

"Thy word my life, Admiral." The boat halted in the sky, and behind it, the others did also, forming a vast ampitheater in the air, with the valley below as the stage. Comedy or tragedy? It was one to the Lorsii.

The admiral postured *sharing of honors.* "Have the princes and captains join me, if they care to."

The information went out, and Lorsii fluttered to the admiral's boat. Among them were concubines and message-bearers from a few captains, begging leave to stay with their crews. One came from Kojja-Je to say that the captain would stay with his wingmate, who was auguring a poem on the passing below. The admiral granted leave, but he was displeased. He had particularly wanted Hass-Ka-Ve beside him: her and her new-found power. Was it possible that she was to be one of those among the Great People, rare as a winter wine, whose *krra* would truly shape the future? Fegge-Gae shook himself mentally. He was becoming as superstitious as an eggling. Nonetheless, he felt a disconcerting loneness.

* * * *

Rebecca Martin paced back and forth along the wooden rampart which had been erected across the middle of the valley as a kind of command post. All around her, laserbeams cut the air, bullets whined, and smoke eddied. Her hands stroked her rifle in frustration. Father Josiah had strictly forbidden the people to fight back and had charged her with maintaining that order. Already, the lower end of the valley was being overrun with zombies. They had clawed their way to the earthen wall through the passive traps and snares the people had set, and had flowed over that wall like dark scum—cautiously, obviously perplexed by the sullen Christians who fell back slowly but offered no resistance.

A bullet struck a lashed pole beside her, sending splinters into her thigh. "That does it," she cried. "Damn you to hell!" She raised the rifle and fired.

Instantly, the Christians joined her, and the valley turned into an inferno. Somewhere, amid the screams of pain and shouts of anger, someone with a deep voice began to sing "Onward Christian Soldiers," and it was taken up until the roll of it beat down the valley like a drum. It seemed to have a physical presence, and the zombie horde slowed, as if outnumbered despite their half-million strength. Then one among them began Zlotny's obscene hymn, and it roared upward in a counterwave of sound. After a time, it seemed as if the bullets and laserbeams were incidental, as if the battle were being fought with song alone.

But song did not kill, and bullets did. Christians were falling in scores and hundreds all over the ever-shrinking perimeter of their defenses. It was only a matter of time—and not much of that. One by one, hard-pressed Christians began looking hopefully toward the tiny church. The hymn they sang became interspersed with cries of "Father Josiah! Father Josiah!"

And at last, he stepped forth, robed all in white and with his staff in his hand. The shout which went up filled the air. Josiah stood on the broken step of the church, looking with sadness over the death and destruction coming up the valley. He did not speak.

Gradually, the firing and noise died away. Even the zombies stood in silence. Every human in the valley knew, somehow, that this old man was beyond their power to help or hinder. With a hundred thousand weapons pointed at him, not a finger pressed a trigger or firing stud.

Josiah raised his staff. "Christians! Lay down your weapons!"

There was a murmur of disbelief, which swelled to an angry chorus.

Josiah stamped the butt of his staff on the ground. "Have you lost faith now, my sons and daughters? Has God yet abandoned you? I say to you now, lay down your arms!"

And they did, hesitantly, fearfully. Those nearest the front lines of the zombies laid their weapons carefully in reach and glared at their adversaries.

One of the zombies grinned wolfishly and raised his weapon toward Crick. Six hundred yards away, the old man looked at him, and he lowered the rifle as if it were too heavy for him to hold.

Crick came down the valley, and the people parted before him. He came to the lines of the zombies and stood in front of those black-clad troops with his old head high. "What do you want here?" he demanded. "Do you come among the people of the Lord God with evil in your hearts?" His staff swung across the lines, and the zombies cringed as it passed. Then the staff pointed skyward, at the Great Boats floating high. "Or do you come in fear of the false masters yonder? You have lived their kind of lives now, and what have you accomplished? Are you happier? Are your parents and sons and daughters happy? Is ruination the way you wish to live out the rest of your lives?" He looked from face to face. Some stared defiantly back, but many dropped their eyes. "Is this the message Jesus Christ died to bring to mankind: kill, burn, loot?" He grounded the point of his staff. "Come to this spot, each of you. Lay down your weapons and your sins. Come among your brothers and be born again into the light of God." He said it quietly, not as a command but an invitation.

There was a terrible tension in the air. Here and there, one among the Zlotnyites started forward, only to be grabbed and held back by others. One broke free and walked nervously toward Josiah, her pistol held above her head by the barrel. Josiah smiled and opened his arms.

"Noooooo!" It was a wail of purest horror, and it came from the throat of Jon Paterson, who was several meters to Father Josiah's left. As thousands of heads turned to him, they saw him staring wild-eyed past Josiah, and they swung their eyes to follow his gaze.

A figure had arisen from a heap of bloody bodies; emaciated, its face frozen in a rictus of malice. It moved with the swiftness of a snake, straight for the patriarch. Even as a score of Christians flung themselves upon it, the figure raised a long, slim dagger and plunged it into Father Josiah's breast.

Josiah staggered back, stumbled, and fell. Even as his legs went weak beneath him, he cried out, "Don't hurt him!"

Paterson and Rebecca were beside the old man almost before he hit the ground, Paterson working feverishly to rip open Crick's robe and stanch the flow of blood. "Don't die," he gritted. "Don't die, Captain."

Crick smiled weakly up at him. "I think you'd better save Mister Zlotny from our brothers' wrath, Jon."

"Zlotny!" Paterson leapt up. He ran to the writhing figure pinned to the ground, and saw that it was, indeed, the fanatic. "Oh, you bastard!" He yanked the self-made evangelist out of the clutch of hands and stood him upright.

Zlotny's face was suffused with rapture. "You can't hurt me, you know. I have served my master, and the Left Hand protects me." He giggled, saliva dribbling down his chin. "I'll live forever, you see. Live forever."

Paterson's hatred left him. He had been too close to insanity himself. He stood as if rooted as Zlotny broke free and ran into the open space between the Christians and the zombies.

"Ye faithful," Zlotny called. "See how the Duality triumphs! See the power we have! Don't you recognize me? Zlotny! The Great Servant! Rise up, ye faithful, smite thy enemies."

But the zombies weren't watching him. Josiah Crick had staggered to his feet, brushing off Rebecca and the Christians who strove to make him lie still. His white robe was bloodied from the heart to the waist, but somehow he seemed stronger and more whole than anyone on the field of battle. He raised his staff and called in a powerful voice. "Ibrihim Zlotny, face me!"

The zealot turned, and a squeak of fear came from him. He backed away from Crick's fierce gaze, shaking his head and gibbering.

Crick's face was a storm and his eyes were lightning. "Do not fear me, Ibrihim Zlotny. I am but a tool of Him who demands payment for your sins." He raised his eyes to heaven. "Father, if it be Thy will—"

On a rise behind the wooden rampart, Hezekiah huddled in fear and shock, the mouse Beelzebub riding his back, buried deep in the cat's fur. The animals had fled the church as fire and sound beat upon them, and had sought sanctuary beneath the cluster of vehicles which had been parked out of the way. Something had registered, perhaps, in the cat's memory, and he had bounded aboard one of the several freightliners among the vehicles. He sought now his familiar perch above the windshield, leaping first on the command chair, then on a ration box Zlotny had set on the dashboard. Hezekiah's weight tipped the box and it fell against the tractor protection valve, releasing the brakes. The *Milk & Honey* began rolling down the slope, gathering speed....

Ibrihim Zlotny hunched over, as if awaiting a stroke of lightning. When it didn't come, he straightened, and in his mad eyes was a light of triumph. "So, Crick! Is that the best your right hand can do?" He swung to the zombies. "See! There is no power save in the Duality. Come, let us—"

The *Milk & Honey* smashed through the wooden rampart, slewed around to the left, and flipped into the air. Her forty kilotons' weight seemed almost buoyant as it arched with implacable grace and came down on Ibrihim Zlotny. But its striking could be felt a thousand meters away. One clawed hand protruded from beneath the impacted cabin. Its fingers curled slowly, then were still. A dazed Hezekiah, the mouse still clinging to his fur, leapt over the hand and scampered away.

* * * *

Aboard the Great Boat, the Lorsii princes and captains chittered and fluttered, an odor of uncertainty and dis-ease coming off them. Fegge-Gae sensed the potential of the mood and made the form for *wagering with merriment*. "Well, my eggmates, it seems that chance sides with the Krrikk again, though it costs him his life. Should there be a poem to the beast?"

"A poem to our lost beast-toy, perhaps?" This from a princeling who was fond of Zlotny.

"Poems are not made to those who lose," the admiral replied, his posture reflecting *slight contempt of an inferior*.

A captain, an admiral in his own right, tilted his wings to catch the setting sun at an angle of superb beauty. "Does the Grand

Admiral still feel it is *Kllua* alone, mere chance, which guides events among the beasts?" His tone was respectful, friendly. But his posture stated *challenge to authority.* "Our near-Srra, the Lady Hass-Ka-Ve, feels that there is a song in those hmmnns, a song with new words, perhaps."

Fegge-Gae's own tone was amused and tolerant, but his odor was one of dangerous warning. "The Lady Hass-Ka-Ve gathers much wisdom in one short session in the Chambers, or so it appears. I recall that the Sage Of Ten Thousand Years, the Prince Pykk-Vle-Srra, was five times in the innermost Chamber before he thought wisdom might possibly have touched him in passing." The admiral shifted his form a bit. "Nonetheless, the Lady has much beauty about her, and should not be dismissed lightly. Let us therefore make wager on her wisdom, shall we?"

The other admiral bowed politely, noting with ungracious admiration how neatly Fegge-Gae had set up to dispose of his challenge. Should he refuse, or should Hass-Ka-Ve be proven wrong, then he would be forever shunned from the highest crags for having been made a fool of. "Very well," he said smoothly, "let us wager something of worth."

"Thou, then?"

"Let us wager, Master of my Nest, thy personal strength against the wisdom of the Lady. Let us wager that thou go among the beasts and personally drink the life of this Krrikk."

All *krra* among the Lorsii on the bridge were tuned to the nuances of this elegant battle. Comment and counter-comment formed as they shifted position and odor among them. Should Fegge-Gae prove victorious, his victory would, after all, be over a mere beast, and neither the Lady Hass-Ka-Ve nor the challenging admiral would suffer for it. Should he lose, the admiral would gain much power from having maneuvered him into the trap.

"A—ah—noble plan," Fegge-Gae said, acknowledging the other's adroitness. "Let us, to insure that the proper songs and sung afterward, take along a master poet as witness. Yourself, perhaps?"

"My Lord honors me," the challenging admiral said, realizing he'd been outfoxed. Win or lose, Fegge-Gae would take him with him.

Fegge-Gae's wings and thorax assumed the form for *entering into history.* "Let it thus be recorded and spoken among our peoples." He signaled the helmsman negligently. "Take us among the beasts."

* * * *

The zombies began to retreat, their eyes riveted on the

overturned freightliner. The Christians almost ignored them, ringing themselves around Father Josiah, who was being carried away on a stretcher. Rebecca walked along beside her grandfather, crying bitterly and kneading his old hand in hers. "Oh, Grandpa," she wept, her voice like a broken thing.

Crick smiled up at her through his pain. "Save your tears, child. I am content. My work is done."

Paterson, walking on the other side of the stretcher, glowered. "It's not. It can't be. That's not the way I saw it."

Crick turned his eyes to Paterson. "It isn't your visions or mine which say when we die, Jon. I'll go when the Lord calls me—and I think that'll be soon, now."

"Oh, Poppa-Bear," Rebecca cried. "Don't say that."

Josiah coughed and winced. "Didn't remember it hurting so much, last time I got stabbed. That was back in '29, on the Mississippi overland run. Fellow resented my bringin' the Word to this saloon, see—"

Paterson wasn't listening. The vast mob of people had all stopped, zombie and Christian alike, and were watching the sky, where admiral Fegge-Gae's Great Boat was descending on them.

Paterson gripped Crick's shoulder. "Look, Captain. Here come the Lorsii. You're not done yet."

"Yes, I am. Jon. This part is up to you."

Paterson's jaw dropped. "N-no. What can I do?"

Rebecca Martin growled at him. "Do any damn thing you want, Paterson, but leave Grandpa alone. You've done enough to kill him as it is."

"Now, child, don't say that about Jon."

The girl glanced at the Christians, who were looking hopefully toward their prostrate leader. "Brothers and Sisters," she cried. "Stand aside. Let the bugs' bootlicker face them!"

A rustle of agreement went through the crowd, and Paterson found himself propelled down the valley by hard hands. The Christians then fled after the stretcher, leaving him alone on the burnt ground, facing the zombies a quarter kilo away and the Great Boat above. He took a shaky breath.

The belly of the Great Boat opened and two Lorsii fell leisurely from it, snapping their wings open at the last moment and skimming across the heads of the zombies, who cheered them. They backed and filled and dropped to a landing a body-length in front of Paterson. The taller one spoke in a high, brittle voice. "So, hmmnn; where Krrikk-beast?"

Paterson could not marshal his thoughts. His mind was filled with hatred, fear, and a strange kind of sympathy he could neither define nor defend. It had something to do with his own belief in his visions, and the irony of these powerful creatures being doomed to defeat. How did he know that? The vision was going wrong already. Crick was dying. Fear/fear/fear.

Paterson set his jaw. "Get back in your damned ship and go. You're beaten."

Both Lorsii made the form for *general amusement*. "Toys beaten, not Lorsii. You stop other beasts. You not stop Lorsii. Lorsii the Great People. Kill all. Kill you, Man."

Paterson felt the hair rise on his neck. Except for the setting, it was a replay of his vision. "Father Josiah stopped your zombies, and your nasty little henchman. *I* got away from you. And if you don't leave, you'll not get away from *me*." He knew the Lorsii could read his emotions, could see the electromagnetic waves emanating from him as an aura. And he also knew, with a kind of astonishment, that that aura was radiating an absolute belief in the reality of what he had just said. Something, someone, had touched him deep inside. And for that moment at least, he was utterly confident of his ability to destroy the aliens. The shorter of the Lorsii made a motion beneath his wing and brought forth an object. He flicked it and it snapped open to become a curious bow. He raised it, aiming at Jon Paterson's face. "Kill you now, Man."

Paterson felt the haloed, singing separation of self from body that had come with each of his visions. He stared into the faceted eyes of the insectoid creature as though it were transparent. Disdainfully, he turned his back. On the ground lay Josiah Crick's staff. He picked it up. "Last chance," he said softly.

Fegge-Gae reached over and pushed his companion's bow aside. "Show power, hmmnn," he said, his *krra* lifted on the sliced edge of the moment. "In name of Great People, I challenge you. Kill if you can!" He unfurled his gorgeous wings and stood like a giant bat on the twilit ground, defiance and deadly menace in every line of his being.

Paterson felt his confidence waver. He licked his lips. What would Crick do?

He raised the staff shakily skyward and took a breath, preparing for a mighty pronouncement. But when the words came out, they were as humble as the voice itself. "Okay, Boss," Paterson said meekly. "Do Your stuff."

The entire valley was silent again, as quiet as death itself. For a long heartbeat, nothing at all happened.

There was a flash in the eastern sky. A piercing bolt of light leapt from the horizon, arrowed through the twilight, and struck the Great Boat, atomizing it. A heartbeat later, the sonic boom hit the ancient mountains, flattening trees, people, and the tiny church with a fist of sound almost beyond comprehension. And when it was gone, nothing moved in the valley. Christian and zombie alike lay prone on the land, and the two Lorsii were shattered like glass goblins.

CHAPTER NINETEEN

In God's heaven, the stars moved in their courses, the universe, busy with being born hither, was equally busy dying yon. Galaxies whirled and tilted and gave up their heat to unending entropy. And in an insignificant galaxy, an insignificant planet whirled around an insignificant star. And on the other side of the star from the planet, the Great Boats of the Lorsii hung in the void, pacing the far planet with watchmaker's precision to keep the fiery sun between it and them.

It took a week for the stately, deadly minuet of ego-battle between the captains and admirals to precipitate out a new Grand Admiral. And when the power-dance was over, the ritual indentures and suicides completed and sung about, the new poems added to the *krra* of the race, it was Kojja-Je who sat on the ruby throne of the late Fegge-Gae. It was he who ordered that Fegge-Gae's name be obliterated from the memory of the Great People, for the shame his failure brought on it. It was he who ordered that every Lorsii in the fleet rip out his or her jewels of power, that they might return home with their shame a banner for all to see. It was Kojja-Je who ordered every eggling in every creche cast into the void, that every line represented on the voyage should be terminated with the now-living representatives. It was he who publicly took responsibility for the disaster, and with his own hands tore from his wings the jewels.

For by these measures of contrition, Kojja-Je hoped to avoid the wrath of the Emperor and escape with at least his life.

And it was Kojja-Je who received Hass-Ka-Ve, not as his wingmate, or as a near-Srra, but as a commanded concubine and ego-slave. He stared at her from the height of the admiral's crag as she knelt on the ice below. "So, Thou of Many Convolutions, thou whose 'wisdom' has blackened the Lorsii name to the ends of time. What would you have of your humble wingmate?"

Her posture was an entirely new form, *submission to someone of no worth.* "I have come to beg a favor."

"Thy favors are costly to the Great People." He flicked his wingtips in a deliberately ungraceful manner. "Would you have me fetch for thee again, as a trained Corra-Ka?"

"Something like that," she said placidly.

Kojja-Je's posture was rigid with repressed fury. "Not that beast!"

"We should take him to Joyworld, My Admiral. He has a song. Our people must know it."

"Never!"

"And if the Emperor wished it?"

The Grand Admiral was off his crag, swooping down on her like a striking hawk. He pulled up with a heavy wrenching of his wings and hit the ice insultingly close to her. "Thou fliest in dangerous airs, Lady. Thou wouldst presume to take a tale to the Emperor?"

"I ask a simple favor of my wingmate," she replied, her neck still exposed in submission. "In memory of shared wines, shared matings."

Kojja-Je's odor became complex. "Ah, yes. Memories. Dost thou recall the last time thou had me fetch thy toy?"

"I do."

"And dost recall my form?"

Her head was almost on the ice. "I do. The four hundred and thirty-third: *this for thee, and my price shall be terrible.*"

Kojja-Je flapped back up to his crag and reclined on the ruby throne. "We leave for Joyworld on the death of the next candle. Thee would have me fetch along Pttrsan." His posture was almost eager. "Even knowing my hatred of the beast? Even knowing that I shall exact a price of thee?"

"Even so."

Kojja-Je leaned back indolently. "Then it shall be done. And my price—?"

The near-Srra wrapped herself in serenity. "My life? It is thine. It always was, wingmate. But thou must make me promise that the Jnn-Pttrsan will come alive to Joyworld, that he will be allowed to speak."

Kojja-Je made the form for agreement. "Indeed, wingmate, I shall do better than that. I shall appoint him a guardian to see that he comes to no harm. *Thou*, to guard him."

Hass-Ka-Ve sat folded into herself on the icy floor of the throne room, a small part of her being, her—*soull*, rejoicing in the knowledge that Pttrsan's song would be sung, that the new thing might come to her people. But in spite of her best efforts, her form blurred, for the major part of her being knew, at last, how very terrible Kojja-Je's price was to be.

* * * *

Charlotte Honesdale found Rebecca, as expected, beside her grandfather's grave. The burial plot was already showing signs of turning into a shrine; someone had started a low brick wall around it, and offerings of flowers carpeted the ground for meters around. Amid the sweet color of the mountain flowers, Rebecca Martin's pale whiteness emphasized her fragility. Charlotte dropped to the ground beside her and sat in silence, sharing the girl's pain.

Rebecca finally looked around. "Hello, Sister Charlotte. How goes it below?" It was obvious that she was being polite for politeness' sake, that her wound was still too fresh. There was clay beneath her fingernails from her stroking of the grave.

The ex-American Secretary replied in kind. "Fairly well. The President is busy organizing everything. He's good at that. It's amazing how rapidly the earth heals itself, isn't it? Look how peaceful the valley is now."

Rebecca nodded, but did not look at the bustle going on in the rapidly rising town—already being called City of Triumph. "They tell me the Zlotnyites are disbanding all over the world."

"Most of them, yes. But we'll be years flushing them all out. Once the brute is given rein in some people, it cannot be controlled except by force."

"More killing," Rebecca said, bitterness and resignation in her voice. "Always more killing."

The black woman sighed. "I've come to ask your help in something, Sister Becky. Jon Paterson—"

"Don't mention that man to me!"

"—Jon Paterson says the Lorsii are coming back."

Rebecca spat. "Of course they are! They'll go home and get the rest of their vile breed, then come back and turn the earth into a cinder. We all know that."

Honesdale shook her head. "Paterson says that they haven't gone home yet, that they're out there waiting. They're coming to pick him up."

"That figures. He's been a loyal puppet for them. Maybe they'll give him a planet to destroy all by himself this time."

"Becky, have charity. He stood up to them, didn't he?"

"God stopped them."

"Yes." Honesdale said it with quiet conviction, causing Rebecca to look closely at her. "And we've got to convince Jon of that before they take him to their world." She leaned forward and took the girl's arm. "Rebecca, don't you see it? The Lord would not have visited all this on us without purpose, would He? And what other purpose could He have than that we bring the Word to them?"

Rebecca recoiled. "I can't believe that those creatures are God's."

"Becky, everything is God's. Even demons." She pointed across the valley. "Jon's over there right now with the President. Falstrom's been pumping him full of science, trying to work up a defense against the Lorsii. And Jon's a scientist, too. He's made himself believe in a scientific explanation for everything that's happened— trying to hide his fear of being taken away. He's even managed to ignore all his visions." She got to her feet. "And we've got to show him that he's wrong and that Father Josiah was right. We've got to send him off armed in the Lord. In that and that alone lies the future salvation of mankind. Only if Jon can bring them morality will they spare us."

Rebecca studied the earnest black woman, then got to her feet. "I didn't take you for so much of a Christian, Sister Charlotte."

Secretary Honesdale smiled shyly. "I've always been what you'd call a 'closet believer.' Now, I'm out of the closet." She held out her hand. "Will you help?"

Rebecca Martin stood silent for a very long time. When she spoke, she measured her words. "Sister Charlotte, Grandpa always accused me of being in love with Jon Paterson, and I guess he was right. But I hate him, too, in spite of God and everybody. I hate him for being in my life, and for my grandfather's death and for things I can't even define. I hate him most of all for coming along either too late or too early, and taking my dreams with him." She took Honesdale's hand. "But I will help if I can."

Together, the two women went down the hill, arm in arm.

* * * *

The Great Boats aligned themselves in the void, each in place to a precision of millimeters. The form was perfect, the comment exquisite, the very beauty of the arrangement enough to power the vessels.

Aboard, the Lorsii raised the poem, passing it from hearts to hearts, wingbeat to wingbeat, until it resonated on frequencies unknown in nature. The *krra* of the Great People blended, amplified, cohered.

And the Great Boats winked out one by one, already halfway home.

Save the flagship. On wings of atomic fire, it flirted the edge of the sun and dove for the third planet out....

* * * *

Jon Paterson had his back to the burnt tree, as if to defend himself. His face was set in lines of stubbornness and fear. Lars Falstrom stood nearby, his own face turned away but equally stubborn. Rebecca Martin and Charlotte Honesdale were facing Paterson, a meter or so away, their faces frustrated. The silence had gone on for some time.

Charlotte made a small gesture. "Let me try it again, Jon."

"It's no use. I just can't buy it."

"Look, how do you account for the miracles? Do you really believe that electromagnetic disturbances created by the Lorsii caused all those earthquakes and lightning strikes?"

"I find that easier to believe than Divine intervention."

Rebecca snorted. "You mean, you're less scared of the former than the latter." Then she bit her lip. "Oh, damn. I'm sorry, I didn't mean it that way."

"You're right, though," Paterson admitted.

Falstrom stepped over, his face red. "Miss Martin, consider the destruction of that Lorsii ship when Jon waved your grandfather's rod. We've *proven* that it was struck by a piece of that meteor Zlotny's cross was made of. Proven it! Can you deny that, or read Divine handiwork into it?"

Rebecca smiled. "The question isn't the means, Mister President, but the end. The miracle is not that God chose a hunk of rock to do His work with, but that He directed it where it was meant to go. Surely *you* can't believe that all the miracles happened at the right place and time, with absolute selectivity, by chance alone? How does your science explain that?"

Falstrom began a retort, but Paterson's sudden tensing stopped him. "What is it, Jon?"

"They're coming. They'll be here in ten minutes."

"Jon," Rebecca pleaded.

"Paterson, be a scientist!"

Paterson put his hands over his ears. "Stop it! Leave me alone."

He turned his back to them and found himself facing the flattened little church, its crooked steeple and tiny bell oddly upright. He pointed. "I'm going there to think. Call me when they come." He strode away from them with determined steps.

He crawled over the wreckage and sat down amid the broken timbers, his head in his hands. Oh, Lord, I don't want this! I don't want to go. I'm afraid. I'm the wrong one. It was supposed to be Crick, not me. I don't want to die on the ice.

He had exulted, earlier, in the thought that it couldn't be him in the visions, for the man in the nightmares was old, grey, bent. But he had seen himself in a mirror: the past weeks and months had aged him at least ten years, and the man who stared horrified out of the silvered glass was the same man as he who died and died and died on the frozen plain.

He wrestled with it for half an hour, wanting with all his heart to believe the Old Story, to believe that there was a God, and that He was guiding events. But the God in his mind's eye was somehow always the aloof, fearsome face of his father, the bleak old man of his youth, the terror of his childhood ineptitudes. And the scientist in him welled up to stamp out that image, to help him retreat into the comfortable world of measurable, definable things, the world where miracles did not happen and creatures from other planets did not descend to take him away. Oh, Lord, help me. Help me!

What was that? A wind? It had to be wind; the church bell was ringing. But it wasn't moving.

And there came to Jon Paterson something that was, perhaps, a voice, saying: Be strong: I am with you.

And another voice—or was it the same one? Jnn-Pttrsan, I come for thee. Be strong: I am with you.

Oh, God, please. Not yet!

Rebecca was at the wall, silent, pale. "They're here."

The Great Boat rode half a kilometer in the sky. The swanboat lay gracefully in the valley. A tall Lorsii stood on the ground before it, and Paterson recognized him, knew that he would meet him again on a bleak and frozen plain. Knew, though, even as he came forward, that the vision might be altered, for there was a song on the wind, a new song.

But fear was uppermost, and the scientist was in him.

Kojja-Je bowed. "Meet again, Jnn-Pttrsan."

"We meet again, Kojja-Je. May you rot in hell eternally."

"May your eggs be worms, beast." The Grand Admiral made a form which Paterson recognized as *anticipation of intense pleasure.* "You live at request my wingmate. She have quaint belief your ugly bellow have song in it. Maybe amuse Emperor." Kojja-Je odored *preposterous, of course.* "Last time, I help you escape. This time, I guarantee you not. I assign you tender care wingmate herself." He gestured toward the swanboat. "Come, Hass-Ka-Ve. Collect toy."

The swanboat's wing dropped. A collective moan went up from the gathered Christians. Rebecca Martin, directly behind Paterson, gave a small, hurt cry.

Hass-Ka-Ve felt her way over the side of the boat, stumbling, and came toward Paterson with her hands tentatively before her. She was blinded, and her wings were torn out at the roots.

Paterson was totally, utterly numb. In the briefest flash of an instant, he knew what had happened, and what it meant. A creature born in beauty, living for grace; a creature with a mind, doomed never to drink the wine, never to sail the high, cold wind, never even to walk upright again.

And in that particle of a moment, Jon Paterson felt, for the first time in his life, Christian charity: an upwelling of pity and love and protectiveness. He stepped forward and took the groping, alien, clawed hands gently in his own.

Has-Ke-Ve made an awkward attempt at the form for *gratitude with affection.* "Greet you," she said, "Brother in Christ."

Paterson was having trouble seeing through his tears. "And I greet you, Sister." He took her arm and turned her toward the gathering. "Here are many more, Hass-Ka-Ve."

The Lorsii raised her hideously wounded eyes as though she could see. "Greet you, Brother, Sister in Christ," she cried.

There was a ripple through the crowd, a shuffling of feet.

Charlotte Honesdale stepped forward, and Rebecca Martin followed her. "Greetings to you," the black woman said, her voice breaking. She touched the alien face lightly, then took Hass-Ka-Ve's hand and placed it against her own cheek. "Bless you, Sister Haskaveh."

Rebecca Martin came, in turn, to touch and be touched. And after her, the rest of the people in the valley. The Lorsii did not weep, but Paterson could read Hass-Ka-Ve's odor, and the emotions were the same.

Kojja-Je appeared, towering over Paterson. "Enough fool-play. We go boat now."

Paterson looked up at the tall being, and there was a strange look in his eyes. He smiled softly. "Time enough, friend. You and I will have time enough. And I think the Lord and I will show the Great People a thing or two about strength before it's over." He took Sister Hass-Ka-Ve's arm and led her to the swanboat, and there was, somehow, a light about them.

And the dark figure of Kojja-Je followed, as the darkness

always shuffles after the light, and they rose in the pine-scented night, perhaps to live forever.

About the Author:

Roger Lovin, at age 36, has been a cook's helper on a Danish lugger, a bos'n on various tramp steamers, a bouncer, a truck driver and a minister of the Gospel at age 16. He has been a singer, a musician, a painter, a stand-up comic and a fashion designer. In Los Angeles, he was editor-in-chief of *New Library Press*, has written features for the *Los Angeles Times*, the *New York Times*, and the *New Orleans Times Picajune*. *Apostle* is his third book-length work, adapted from a story in *Flame Tree Planet*. He has written *The Complete Motocycle Nomad* (Little, Brown & Co.) and *The Presence* (Fawcett/Gold Medal) under the byline of Rodgers Clemens. A native of East Tennessee, he now lives in New Orleans.